RETURN OF THE SUN

Other Books by Joseph Bruchac

The Road to Black Mountain, 1976, Thorpe
Springs Press, Berkeley, CA.

This Earth is a Drum, 1977, Cold Mountain
Press, Austin, TX.

Entering Onondaga, Cold Mountain Press,
Austin, TX.

The Dreams of Jessie Brown, Cold Mountain
Press, Austin, TX.

There Are No Trees in the Prison, 1978, Black-
berry Press, Brunswick, ME.

Mu'ndu Wi Go, Mohegan Poems, 1978, Blue
Cloud Quarterly, Marvin, SD.

The Good Message of Handsome Lake, 1979,
Unicorn Press, Greensboro, NC.

Translator's Son, 1981, Cross Cultural Communi-
cations Press.

Remembering the Dawn, 1983, Blue Cloud
Quarterly, Marvin, SD.

*Survival This Way: Interviews With American
Indian Poets*, 1987, University of Arizona,
Tucson.

Children's Books

The Wind Eagle and Other Abenaki Stories,
1984, Bowman Books, Greenfield Center, NY.

Iroquois Stories, 1985, The Crossing Press

RETURN OF THE SUN

Native American Tales
From The Northeast Woodlands

by Joseph Bruchac

Illustrations by Gary Carpenter

The Crossing Press
Freedom, California 95019

Cover illustration and design by Gary Carpenter
Interior illustrations by Gary Carpenter

Printed in the U.S.A.

Library of Congress Cataloging-in-Publication Data

Bruchac, Joseph, 1942–
        Return of the sun.
        1. Woodland Indians—Legends.   2. Indians of North
American—Northeastern States—Legends.   I. Title
E78.E2B78 1989   398.2'08997   88-35197
ISBN 0-89594-344-1   --   ISBN 0-89594-343-3 (pbk.)

TABLE OF CONTENTS

Introduction

Stories are the life of a people. They tell of the deepest hopes and fears of a nation. They reflect both everyday life and dreams. They affirm and help to sustain the values of a culture. This is especially true of the traditional tales of the various Native American nations of the area which has been loosely described as the "Northeastern Woodlands," that area between the Great Lakes and the Atlantic Ocean which includes the present New England states, New York, Pennsylvania, and parts of Canada. In the old days, the artificial boundaries of the states and national borders which affect our perceptions today did not exist. Instead, the people perceived themselves in relation to the natural world, the watersheds of streams, the shores of the great ocean, the hills and mountains of the land. Their ways of life revolved around an intimate knowledge of the animals and plants, the techniques for survival which made their lives good. It was as natural for Native Americans then (and many Native Americans still) to be as familiar with the bounty of the forest or the sea—its store of food and medicine items—as we are with the sections in a supermarket or the stores in a shopping mall. Their stories reflected and helped imbue that knowledge.

Although there were dozens of distinct tribal nations, virtually all of the peoples of the northeast belonged to one of two great language families. Those many peoples who spoke varieties of the Algonquin language were found further to the east of the Hudson River while the speakers of that other great family of languages which we call Iroquoian lived primarily to the west of Lake Champlain in the north and the Hudson River to the south. The

Algonquin languages and the Iroquoian languages are as different from each other as English from Chinese, but their differing tongues were no barrier to trade. There is plenty of evidence, both in archaeology and in the accounts of the early European settlers in the 16th and 17th centuries, to indicate that people and goods traveled widely throughout North America. Their means of subsistence were diverse—witness the Abenaki peoples of the seashores with their emphasis on the many harvests from the ocean versus the agricultural Seneca people of the area south of Lake Ontario with their dependence upon the Three Sisters: Corn, Squash and Beans. The Five (and later Six) Nations of the Iroquois League—Mohawk, Cayuga, Oneida, Onondaga and Seneca—formed a great league of nations, with a constitution which appears to have had a direct influence in the framing of the Constitution of the United States of America. The Five Nations often lived in very large villages made up of longhouses which might hold twenty or more different families in separate apartments around the central fires. The Western Abenaki people lived in small hunting bands of a few families, migrating seasonally to follow the game animals, to go where the fish were running, to camp near the berry patches. There were great differences. There were also many similarities. In most of the nations, women held a central and influential place. They controlled the households and the fields. They chose the leaders among the Iroquois, and among the Algonquins there were sometimes women chiefs. Men were usually the hunters and defenders of their people, using their strength when it was needed, but often deferring to the judgment of the older women. Children were treated with great forbearance by elders, allowed the freedom to "roam wild," while also playing a role in the life of the people which encouraged them to learn the skills and traditions of their nations through direct experience, through imitating their elders, through taking part. The animals and the plants were not viewed as commodities, but as separate and equal nations which deserved and were given respect. Human beings were not all-powerful. As Howard Russell put it in his informative book *Indian New England Before the Mayflower*: "To the Indian the whole creation was replete with powers: the sun, the moon, the four winds, thunder, rain; in his own person, the heart, the lungs. Often mysterious in their actions, the forces of nature could not be controlled directly by man, but respect and ceremony might influence and appease them." The earliest European accounts of Native American people of the Northeastern Woodlands almost uniformly describe them as people who were healthy (prior to the introduction of European diseases), well proportioned, tall, and handsome people. Giovanni Verrazano, the Italian navigator, described the people of the New England coast in the early 1500s as follows: "This is the goodliest people and of the fairest condition that we have found on our voyage; they exceed us in bigness, they are the color of brass, some of them incline more to whiteness, others are of a yellow color, with long and black hair which they are careful to turn out and deck up: they are of a sweet and pleasant countenance."

The native cultures of the northeast existed in balance with their surroundings, but there was also much borrowing from one culture to the next. Material goods—and stories—traveled freely among the native nations of pre-Columbian times. It appears that continuous, large-scale warfare between the peoples of the Northeastern Woodlands was introduced by the Europeans when they imported the rivalry between the British and French, forcing various Native American nations to take sides.

There are stories which came out of those later years of conflict, but the tales which make up this collection are different from those. (It should be noted, however, that the Tuscarora people, though Iroquoian, were found until the 18th century in the area which is now North Carolina. Forced from their lands by the whites, they were given sanctuary by their cousin nations of the Iroquois confederacy and today have a reservation near Niagara Falls.) These are stories—with only one exception—which have ancient roots. One of the oldest of these may be The Walum Olum or "Red Score" of the Lenni Lenape people, which was recorded in glyphs drawn on pieces of wood. Pictographic writing is found throughout North America. In New England, for example, petroglyphs are found in such places as Bellows Falls in Vermont, Dighton Rock in southern Massachusetts, and on rock faces in Rhode Island. Picture writing on trees or rocks to mark hunting territories or leave messages was common in Maine among the Penobscots. Although the original pieces of wood on which The

Walum Olum was recorded no longer exist, Lenape elders in New Jersey and Oklahoma (where many Lenape were relocated by force during the 1800s) accept its authenticity. The story it tells is very similar to other creation stories among Algonquin speaking peoples. It is offered here not only in translation, but with the original glyphs and the Lenape language.

As in The Walum Olum, the emphasis in many of these stories is on peace and balanced relations, both among human beings and between humans and the natural world. When that balance is upset—as in the Tuscarora story of "Why People Speak Many Tongues"—the consequences are always unpleasant. Some of these stories are so ancient that they are found—in various forms—among many different Native American nations. In fact, in choosing the various tellings of these stories, I have often had to decide whether to tell an Abenaki version or a Mohawk one, a Lenape version or a version found among the Seneca. I have not approached these stories as an ethnologist or a folklorist. Instead, I have responded to them as a person of Indian ancestry who has found himself taught and guided by such stories for most of his life.

As in previous collections, I have chosen not to tell the stories I know which have yet to appear in print. Other versions of each of the stories in this book can be found printed in other places—such as Frank G. Speck's *Penobscot Tales and Religious Beliefs*, *Seneca Fiction, Legends, and Myths* collected by Jeremiah Curtin and J.N.B. Hewitt, Horace Beck's *Gluskap The Liar*, and Arthur Parker's *Rumbling Wings*. I know a number of Native American storytellers who continue to deliberately refrain from writing down stories they know because they wish them to remain in the oral tradition, sometimes in their original languages. The traditional time for telling these stories in the Northeast—among virtually all the various tribal nations—was between first frost and last frost. Keeping those stories not yet recorded in writing as part of their own oral tradition alone is seen by some Native Americans as a way to keep those stories pure and strong. I respect that feeling and trust that the oral tradition is at least as lasting as words written on paper. Thus, there are no "new" stories here.

However, my own tellings of these may be seen to differ considerably from other collected versions. I approach writing down my own version of a story by following a number of steps. For one, in a number of cases, I have gone back to the original language—Seneca in some cases, Penobscot or Passamaquoddy or Mohican or Western Abenaki in others—and retranslated the tales. Through my experience with the way Native American people speak—whether English or an indigenous tongue—I have attempted to make the rhythms of the stories match that native way of speaking more closely. I tell my own version of a story only after I have lived with it for a long time. In some cases, I have been given permission by an individual Native teller to tell a story, but I have been asked not to write a version of it down. In such cases, I have always honored that request. Though each of these stories has come to me, at least in part, through living oral traditions (with the exception of The Walum Olum), I have augmented that with considerable research into the written versions of that story. Moreover, I have tried to visit the places where those stories are by tradition supposed to have taken place. A special understanding of a story develops through holding it in your mind for a long time before trying to tell it, through knowing living people whose ancestors passed that tradition on to them, through seeing the place where that story takes place, through a subjective relationship with that story which develops in such nonrational (by western standards) channels as in dreams. Because of this, I limit my storytelling to the northeast, to places where I have walked and to stories which are connected to me through land and blood.

There are still many Native American storytellers. Those who have been especially generous to me and to others here in the northeast include Ray Tehanetorens Fadden (Mohawk), whose Six Nations Indian Museum is found in the Adirondack mountains of New York State; the late Princess Red Wing (Wampanoag/Narragansett) of Rhode Island; the late Mdawilasis Maurice Dennis (Abenaki) of Old Forge, New York, and Odanak, Quebec; and Gladys Tantaquidgeon (Mohegan) who runs the Mohegan Indian Museum in Uncasville, Connecticut. There are, however, many others. A recent book entitled *Spirit of the New England Tribes* by William S. Simmons studies Indian History and Folklore from 1620 through 1984 and concludes, among other things, that it is in the continuing folklore of the New England Native peoples that their spirit and their Indian identity have most strongly survived. They can, perhaps, be best understood through their stories—past and present. It is my hope that *Return of the Sun* will foster a better understanding and appreciation of the wonderful legacy which the Native people of the Northeast offer— to both Indian and non-Indian alike—in the form of lesson stories which instruct and delight, which explain and sustain. Now, more than ever before, we need these teachings which lead us towards peace with each other, respect for the earth, and understanding of the sacred nature of that greatest gift, which is nurtured by the sun whose return each day must never be taken for granted—the gift of life itself.

Daylight shone all around them as they pulled their canoe up on the shore of the island.

The Return of the Sun
(Onondaga)

Long ago, the People of the Longhouse say, the Sky Woman, fell to earth through a hole in the Sky Land made by the uprooting of the Great Tree. That tree was uprooted because she had a dream in which she saw the tree lying on its side. When Sky Woman fell, she was already expecting a child. The geese caught her between their wings and brought her gently down to the new earth which had been made for her on the back of the Great Turtle. There, she gave birth to a daughter, the first person born on Earth.

That daughter had twin sons, fathered by the West Wind. One of those sons was the Good Mind, the other was the one called Flint. The Good Mind was born in the proper way, but Flint forced his way out of his mother's side, killing her. Then he told his Grandmother, Sky Woman, that it was his brother, the Good Mind, who caused their mother's death.

Because of this, Ataensic, Sky Woman, was very

2

angry at the Good Mind. She always took his brother's side, even though Flint's mind was full of bad thoughts. When his brother did things which made the earth a better place, Flint did things which made life hard.

After the death of their mother, Ataensic talked with her two grandsons about what to do so that their mother would be remembered.

"Let us place her head in the sky," Flint said. "Then it will always remind those on earth of what came to pass."

"That is good," Ataensic said. She placed her daughter's head in the sky and it became the Sun, looking down on the world.

"Let us make it so that my dear mother's head will do good for the world," Good Mind said. "Let it be her duty to bring light and warmth to the days. It will help the plants to grow and make life possible for the human beings to come."

"I do not agree," Flint said. "It is enough to place my mother high in the sky so that no one can touch her. Some of those to come might even try to steal her from the sky. It will be better if there are no green things on this earth. Then nothing can continue to live here and my mother's head will be safe."

The Good Mind did not agree with this, but Sky Woman took the part of Flint. So it was decided that the Good Mind and his Grandmother would have a contest. They would play a game by placing into a bowl six peach stones painted half black and half

3

white. They would shake the bowl and determine the winner by the way the stones came up. If Sky Woman won, all of the green things on Earth would cease to grow. If the Good Mind won, then the Sun would shine down from the sky and the life of the animals and the human beings to come would be possible. The game would be played after the passing of ten days.

The Good Mind went back to his lodge. There he spoke to the animals and the birds. He said, "It has been arranged that I must play a game against my Grandmother. If she wins this game, then all life on Earth will soon end. If I win, then life will continue. If I ask you to assist me, will you help?"

All of the animals and birds agreed.

Then the Good Mind spoke to the chickadees. "I will need help from six of you." Immediately, all of the chickadees came to him in a flock. They perched singing on his arms. He chose six and borrowed their heads from them, for their heads were half black and half white and shaped just like the stones for the bowl game.

After ten days had passed, Sky Woman came to the Good Mind's Lodge. Sky Woman had brought her own bowl and stones.

"Grandmother," the Good Mind said, "We will play with your bowl, but we must use my stones." Then he placed into the bowl the heads of the six chickadees. "Now, Grandmother," he said, "throw the bowl first."

Sky Woman took the bowl. She shook it and then

4

threw the stones high into the air. "Three," she called, "let three come together!" The six stones, which were the heads of the chickadees, flew high into the air, singing as they rose. They went high out of sight, though the sounds of their singing could still be heard. "Three," Sky Woman kept saying, "let three come together." Now the six stones, which were the heads of the chickadees, began to fall down. They came into sight still singing. "Three," Sky Woman said again, "Let three come together." But when the six stones landed, they landed with all six of them turned up towards the black side.

"It is my turn, Grandmother," said the Good Mind. He took the bowl and threw the six stones, which were the heads of the chickadees, up into the sky. Again they rose high, singing as they went. Again his Grandmother chanted "Three, let three come together." But when the six stones landed, they landed with all six of them turned up towards the black side.

"Grandmother," said the Good Mind. "I have made a field. I have won this game. Now the life on this earth is out of your hands. All the things which have begun to grow here will continue."

Sky Woman and Flint were not happy. That night, when all was dark, she took the Sun and went with it to her lodge on an island, far to the east. There she hung the Sun on a tree where it could no longer give light to the world.

When three days had passed, the Good Mind

said, "I must go and bring back the Sun. Life cannot continue here on the earth in darkness. I must travel to the east. Who will make a canoe for me?"

"I will do it," said the Beaver. With his sharp teeth, the Beaver cut down a tree. Then the Woodpecker came and hollowed it out.

"Now," said the Good Mind, "who will travel with me?"

"I will travel with you," said the Fisher.

"I will come, also," said the Beaver.

"I will go," said the Otter.

"And I shall come with you, too," said the Fox.

Then they began to travel towards the east. They paddled swiftly and the Beaver steered the canoe with his broad tail. It was very dark, but they kept traveling towards the east. At last, in front of them, they could see a faint glow of light. They paddled harder and it grew lighter still. Now they could see in front of them a wonderful sight. There was an island with a tall tree growing in its center. Held in the top of that tree, tied there to keep it from going back up into the sky, was the Sun. Daylight shone all around them as they pulled their canoe up on the shore of the island.

"We must go quietly and not waken my Grandmother," the Good Mind said. "Who will climb the tree and unfasten the sun?"

"I will do it," said the Fisher. He jumped up into the tree and climbed to the top where the Sun was tied. Then he bit through the bonds which held the Sun. But as he did so, he rattled some of the branches and the Sky Woman woke in her lodge near the base of the tree.

"Who is it?" she called. "Who is trying to steal my daughter's head?"

"Quickly," the Fox called, "throw the Sun down to me."

The Fisher threw down the Sun and Fox caught it in his mouth. Sky Woman tried to grab him, but Fox was too quick. He ran around the island and leaped into the waiting canoe along with the Fisher.

"Now we must all paddle hard," the Good Mind said. "If my dear Grandmother calls to us, do not answer her."

Sky Woman stood on the shore weeping with anger.

"Why have you done this?" she shouted to the Good Mind, but he did not answer or look back.

"Fox," she called, "take pity on an old woman and allow the Sun to come back."

But Fox did not turn around or answer her.

"Fisher," she called, "take pity on an old woman and allow the Sun to come back to me."

But Fisher only paddled harder.

Then she called to the Otter and her power was so strong that he could not resist her. "Otter," she called, "take pity on an old woman and allow the Sun to come back to me."

"So be it," Otter said and he started to turn back towards Sky Woman's island. But Beaver, in the back of the boat, struck Otter in the face with his tail, breaking the spell. He struck Otter so hard that it flattened his face and all otters have flat faces to this day.

They continued on until they reached home. There the Good Mind placed the Sun back into the sky, fastening it firmly so that it could not be brought down ever again.

"My Mother," the Good Mind said, "I have restored you to the sky. Now you will come each day and give the people light and life."

And so it has been ever since. Da ne-ho.

One of the litter, the last one born, was pure white except for a round mark over each of its eyes. There had never before been a dog like that one.

Why The People
Speak Many Tongues
(Tuscarora)

Long ago, back when the world was new, all of the people spoke one language. The minds of those people were good and they lived together in peace. There were not so many people then and their villages were few, but they visited each other often and never fought with their neighbors.

Each of those villages had a leader, one person who was chosen because they were wise and fair. Each of those chiefs helped their people to continue living in harmony. The largest of the villages was beside the great river. The village was so big, in fact, that half of the people lived on one side of the river and half lived on the other side. On one side were the berry fields and the places where people dug roots and found the medicine plants. On the other side the hunting was very good.

In those days, the people had not yet learned to use canoes, so they built a strong bridge from one side of the stream to the other. The bridge was made of the branches of trees and long poles woven tightly together with ropes made of the inner bark of the basswood tree. It arched high above the water so that even the spring floods could not wash it away. The people of both sides used this bridge all the time. They crossed back and forth to trade skins and meat, berries and roots and medicine with each other. On one side of the stream they built their longhouse in which all the people could assemble. So, in the evenings when the drums began to sound, the people crossed back and forth to take part in the dances held each night in the Longhouse.

The people of Big Village were happy. Everyone agreed that the two sides of Big Village were equal. There was nothing that anyone wanted which could not be gotten by trading with their brothers and sisters on the other side of the bridge.

The chief of Big Village was a woman named Godasiyo. She lived on the other side of the stream from the council house and she was regarded as a very good leader by all. It seemed that nothing would ever break the peace of those first people.

One day, though, something happened. Godasiyo, like many of the other people, had several dogs. Those dogs were just like members of the family, with their own names and their special places by the campfire. Godasiyo's favorite dog was a female called "Good One." When Good One had her first litter of seven pups, everyone was both pleased and surprised. They were surprised because one of those seven pups, the last one born, was pure white, except for a round mark over each of its eyes. There had never before been a dog like that one.

"This one," Godasiyo said, "is very special. I shall keep him for myself."

That was where the trouble began. The little white dog was so special that the people on Godasiyo's side of the river began to brag about it.

"There is no dog like ours on your side of the river," they said.

Then the people on the other side began to grow jealous. Soon there were quarrels at the dances in the Longhouse and some of the young men got into fights with each other.

Godasiyo wondered what she could do. She thought of giving the little white dog to someone on the other side of the river. But then, she thought, the people on this side would be jealous. Each day the trouble grew worse and now the two sides of Big Village were almost at war with each other. People no longer crossed back and forth across the bridge. Then one day some of the young men from her side of the river came to her.

"We must destroy the bridge," they said. "We think that those jealous people on the other side are going to come over and steal our white dog."

Then Godasiyo decided. The troubles had gone too far for things to be as they had once been. Before long, the people would begin hurting each other in their fighting. There could no longer be any peace in Big Village. She gathered the people together by the side of the river.

"Things are not good here," she said. "Perhaps we can find peace in a new village. If you wish to come with me, we shall leave and never return."

"But how shall we go?" one of the elders said. "Our enemies from the other side of the stream might follow us."

Godasiyo was ready with her answer. "I have been watching the way pieces of bark float when they fall into the river. On our side there are many birch trees. I think that we will be able to make something from their bark and then use that to go down the river." She looked at her people and sighed. "But first we must destroy the bridge across the river."

The people from her side did as she said. That night they set fire to the bridge and it fell into the stream. The two sides of the village were no longer joined together. Then, all the next day, they worked. They peeled bark from the birch trees and carved pieces of cedar, shaping them like the ribs of a fish to hold the bark covering in place. They sewed the big pieces of birchbark together with strong roots and used pitch from the trees to make them watertight. So they made the first canoes.

Then all of Godasiyo's people gathered their things and made ready to leave. But, even before they set out, they began to quarrel. Everyone wanted to have the honor of carrying their chief and her little white dog. Finally, Godasiyo held up her hand.

"My people," she said, "will this quarreling never end? I see what we must do. I can travel in no one's canoe."

Then she told the people what to do. Taking strong poles, they tied saplings between the two largest canoes. On the space over the water between them, they fashioned a platform. There the Chief would ride with her little white dog.

So they set out on the river, shouting insults at the people left behind on the other bank. They went a long way upstream before they came to a place where the river divided. Some of the people wanted to go up one fork. Some of the people wanted to go up the other. They quarreled with each other and they would not listen as Godasiyo tried to quiet them. Once again, the people were divided, with half wanting to go one way and half wanting to go the other. But which way would their chief and the wonderful little white dog go? They began to fight back and forth. Then the men in the two big canoes each tried to pull the other's boat in their direction. One boat headed to the right. One headed to the left. Suddenly, the platform between the two canoes broke free. Chief Godasiyo and her little white dog fell into the water and sank.

The people pulled their boats together and looked into the river. Their chief was nowhere to be seen, but deep within the water they saw a huge sturgeon swimming away, followed by a little whitefish.

The people in the different boats tried to talk with

each other then, but something strange had happened. They could not understand each other. They were all speaking different languages. So it is to this day. Jealousy and quarreling divided the people and brought many different languages into the world.

*Wunzh rose up and began to wrestle with Mondawmin.
At first he felt weak from his days of fasting, but he grew
stronger as they fought. Just as he was about to throw
Mondawmin, darkness fell as the night heron called.*

The Coming of Corn (Anishinabe)

The people were in need of food. They hunted for game animals and they fished in the streams and the lakes. They gathered nuts and roots and berries and when the wild rice was ripe in the marshes, they went out in the canoes and harvested it. But this was not enough. When the winters were hard and long, the old people and the children suffered. Many began to pray to the Creator for help.

Among them was a young man whose name was Wunzh. Wunzh was very worried about his people. His father and mother were old and he did not know if they could live through another winter. He saw how thin the little children became during the time of deep snows.

So, when the spring returned, he went alone into the forest and made a lodge. Then he sat there without eating or drinking. He kept praying to the Creator, Gitchee Manitou. "My people are hungry," he said. "They are in need of help." He did this for many days, growing weak from hunger and thirst,

17

but he would not give up until he knew Gitchee Manitou heard his prayers.

One evening, as he sat in front of his lodge, Wunzh saw someone coming towards him. It was a tall young man dressed in green. His long hair was as golden as the sun.

"I am Mondawmin," the tall young man said. "Gitchee Manitou has heard your prayers. I have come to help. Now you must wrestle with me."

Wunzh rose up and began to wrestle with Mondawmin. At first he felt weak from his days of fasting, but he grew stronger as they fought. Just as he was about to throw Mondawmin, darkness fell as the night heron called. "We must stop now," Mondawmin said. "I will return tomorrow."

When the next evening came, Mondawmin again appeared. Once more they wrestled and once more Wunzh grew stronger and stronger. However, just as the night before, the cry of the heron and the coming of night ended their contest before he could win.

On the third evening it happened again in the same way. However, as Wunzh slept, Mondawmin appeared in his dream. "Tomorrow," Mondawmin said, "you will defeat me. You will throw me to the ground and kill me. Then you must do as I say if you want to help your people. Strip off my clothing and bury me in the soft earth in a place where the sun and rain can touch my grave. Keep the birds and animals away. Keep the earth loose and let no weeds grow there. If you do this, you will see me again."

When the fourth evening came, Mondawmin returned. Wunzh stood and began to wrestle with him. The tall young man was strong and Wunzh fought hard. They wrestled back and forth, neither one having the advantage. Now it was almost time for the heron to call and the sky was growing dark.

Wunzh gathered all of his strength together. He lifted Mondawmin up and threw him to the ground so hard that his back was broken and he was dead.

Then Wunzh did as he had been told in his dream. He stripped off Mondawmin's green clothing and plumes and buried him in the soft earth where the sun and rain could touch the grave. He kept the earth clean of weeds and kept the birds and animals away. The days passed and something began to grow out of the grave. Shoots as green as Mondawmin's clothing appeared in the soft earth. The summer passed and the new plants grew as tall as a man. As he watched the plants move with the wind, it seemed as if Wunzh could see the figure of Mondawmin dancing among them.

When the fall came, the golden tassels on top of the stalks were the same color as Mondawmin's golden hair. On the side of each stalk grew the ears of corn. One night, Mondawmin again appeared to Wunzh as he dreamed. "Now you must gather the new food which our Creator has given to the people. Pull off the ears on each stalk and strip away the outer husks. Within you will find the new food which will help your people. Never eat all of this food, but always dry some and save it to use during the winter. Keep the best seed for the spring when you will plant it so that you and your children's children will continue to see me each year."

When the next day came, Wunzh did as he was told. He gathered the ears of corn and called the people to join him in a feast. They sang and praised Gitchee Manitou, thanking him for this great gift. So it was that the prayers of the people were answered with the coming of corn.

Fox crawled closer until he was next to a small boy sitting at the edge of the crowd. "Little brother," Fox
whispered, "tell the people that you will get the fire."

How The People Got Fire
(Penobscot)

Long ago, the people had no fire. At first, without fire, their lives were not bad. However, one day, it began to grow colder. The people huddled together and tried to keep warm, but it grew colder still. As the days went on and the cold did not go away, the people saw they would have to do something or they would die. So they called a council meeting.

"We have heard," the elders said, "that there is a thing called fire. It is a dangerous thing, but it can keep us warm."

"Where can we find this fire?" the younger people said.

"We have heard," said the elders, "that fire is kept in a cave by an old woman and her two daughters. They guard the fire from anyone who would steal it and they will give fire to no one. They kill anyone they catch trying to take fire. It will be hard, but someone must go and steal fire or we will not survive. Who is brave enough to go and bring back fire?"

No one spoke. Everyone was afraid. Fox had been listening from the forest near the council circle. He crawled closer until he was next to a small boy sitting at the edge of the crowd.

"Little brother," Fox whispered, "tell the people that you will get the fire."

The boy looked at the Fox, surprised that he had spoken. Then the boy shook his head. "I cannot do it," the boy said.

"Little brother," Fox whispered, "I will help you. With my help, you will surely succeed."

After hearing that, the boy decided. He stood up and stepped forward into the council circle.

"I will go and get fire," he said.

Everyone looked at him and the elders shook their heads. He was such a small boy. "How will you do this?" they said.

"I will go and get fire," the boy said.

"Will no one else go and get fire for the people?" the elders said. No one else volunteered. So, even though they did not think he could do it, they told the boy to go and try.

As soon as the people left the council area, Fox came up to the boy.

"First," Fox said, "you must lay dry sticks together to make a bed for the fire when it is brought back. Then you must get two pairs of good snowshoes. Put one pair on and hang the other about your neck. Then you must run fast and keep running until you can run no more. That is the only way to reach the cave of fire keepers. I will show you the way to go."

The boy gathered dry sticks and piled them together to make a bed for the fire. Then he went and got two strong new pairs of snowshoes. He strapped one pair onto his feet, hung the second pair around his neck, and went to the edge of the woods.

"Now," Fox said, "run as fast as you can. Run in that direction. I will be right behind you."

The boy began to run. He ran as fast as he could. He ran and ran until he thought he could run no more. But as soon as he started to slow up, Fox began to snap at his ankles.

"Run on, Little Brother, run on!" Fox said and the boy kept running. He ran for a long time, but again began to tire. As soon as he slowed down, Fox nipped at his ankles again.

"Run on, Little Brother, run on!" Fox said and then darted in front of the boy. The boy was angry now at Fox. He began to chase him, but Fox stayed just ahead, leading him on. Four times the boy slowed down and four times Fox nipped at his ankles and kept him running.

Finally, the boy could run no more. His snowshoes were worn out. He stopped at the bank of a river. His legs could no longer hold him up and he sank to his knees in the snow.

The Fox came up to him and placed four dry twigs on the ground. "Little Brother," he said, "you have done well. The cave of the keepers of fire is just a little further down this river. Now you must do as I say. Leave your second pair of snowshoes here. Hide these four twigs inside your clothing where they will stay dry. When the keepers of the fire are asleep, then you can light those twigs. After you have done that, stomp out the fire and run back here to your snowshoes. The fire keepers will chase you, but if you do as I say, you will escape."

"I will do as you say," said the boy. He put down the second pair of snowshoes, wrapped the dry twigs in a piece of deerskin and put them inside his clothes. "How will I get into the cave where they keep the fire? Is it not true that the fire keepers kill anyone who tries to get close?"

"Turn yourself into a rabbit," the Fox said. "It is something you can do."

The boy turned himself into a rabbit.

"Now," Fox said, "because you are a rabbit, you must try to escape from me."

The boy who was now a rabbit tried to run away, but Fox was in front of him every way he ran. Finally, because there was no other way to go, he jumped into the river and began to float downstream, struggling in the water. He floated past the cave where the old woman and her two daughters kept the fire. The daughters heard the sound of his splashing and came down to the river to look.

"A rabbit is drowning," one of the sisters said.

"Pull him out," said the other. "We will dry him off by our fire."

Soon, the boy who was now a rabbit, was dry and warm by the fire. He watched the two sisters and the old woman as they tended the fire. It grew later and later in the night and finally the old woman could stay awake no longer.

"Keep watch on the fire," she said. "I can feel that there are thieves nearby." Then she went to sleep.

The two sisters were tired, too. After a time, the older of the two sisters decided she could watch no longer.

"Keep watch on the fire," she said to the younger sister. Then she, too, went to sleep.

Now only the one sister was watching. The boy who was disguised as a rabbit began to hum a sleep song. The younger sister's eyelids grew heavier and heavier. Finally she, too, could stay awake no longer.

"You," she said to the rabbit, "keep watch on the fire while I sleep."

The boy who was disguised as a rabbit waited for a time to make sure all three of the fire keepers were really asleep. Then he changed back into his own shape. He took the first of the four dry sticks and lit it in the fire. Then he stomped on the fire, putting it out. As soon as the fire was out, the old woman and her two daughters woke.

"He is stealing the fire!" the old woman shouted. "Stop him."

The boy ran outside the cave with the three following him. When he reached his snowshoes, he jumped onto them, tied them quickly and began to run. With his snowshoes it was easier for him to run than the firekeepers, but they still kept following. Fox ran alongside him. Now the younger of the two sisters was very close.

"Light the second stick!" Fox shouted.

The boy lit the second dry stick from the first one, which had almost burned out. Then he threw the first stick into the snow to one side. The younger sister stopped to pick it up and the boy kept running. He ran and ran without stopping. Now the older of the two sisters was close behind and almost ready to grab him.

"Light the third stick," Fox shouted.

The boy lit the third dry stick from the second one and threw the second one behind him in the snow. The older sister stopped to pick it up and the boy kept running. He ran and ran without stopping and Fox ran along beside him. The old woman was very close to him now. He could feel her breath on his neck and she reached for him with her long arms.

"Light the fourth stick!" Fox shouted.

Before the old woman could grab him, the boy lit the fourth dry stick and threw the third one behind him. Just like her daughters, the old woman stopped to pick up the stick. Now the boy was getting close to his village. The fourth stick was still burning, but it was very short. The boy was so tired that he could hardly move his legs. He tripped and fell in the snow. Fox, who had been following him, jumped out and grabbed what little was left of the fourth stick in his mouth. It was still burning and it was so short that it burned Fox's mouth. To this day all foxes have black mouths because of that. Fox ran to the place where the sticks were placed to make a bed for the fire. He dropped the ember onto it. The fire blossomed up and all of the people came and gathered around.

That was how the people got fire.

The Bear Clan Mother welcomed the old man, "Dahjoh, Grandfather," she said, "come inside."

The Origin of Medicine
(Tuscarora)

Long ago, an old man dressed in ragged clothes came to a small village. He was sickly and covered with sores. His hair was matted, his face dirty. He went to the door of the first long house. A beaver skin hung over the door indicated that it belonged to the people of the Beaver Clan. It was the custom in those days that anyone who was in need of food or a place to spend the night could come to the door of a lodge and ask freely for help from the head of that household.

Among the Iroquois, it is the Clan Mothers who are the heads of the households. So, when the old man pulled aside the skin hung in front of the door and asked for food, the woman who was head of the Beaver Clan came to the doorway.

"Go away, old man," she said. There was scorn in her voice for his dirty clothes and disgust for his sickness. "We have no food to share."

The old man went next to the lodge where a deer skin above the door tokened that those within were of the Deer Clan. Once again, the woman who was head of the clan turned him from the door.

"Go away, old beggar," the Deer Clan woman said. "Take your sickness elsewhere."

So the old man hobbled to each of the longhouses in the village in turn. He went to the house of the Wolf Clan, the Turtle Clan, and the Heron Clan. All of them drove him from their door and some even threatened him.

At last he came to one longhouse with the skin of a bear over the door, marking it as the Bear Clan's lodge. Before he could speak, the Bear Clan Mother welcomed the old man.

"Dah-joh, Grandfather," she said, "come inside."

She sat the old man by the fire. She cleaned his face and combed his hair and gave him a shirt to wear. She gave him food and while he ate she prepared a bed for him by spreading out skins.

"Grandchild," the old man said, "you must do me one more favor."

Then he instructed her to go into the woods. There, at the base of a certain tree on its northern side, she would find a certain herb growing. She was to leave a small offering of tobacco and then pull up that plant and bring it to him. The woman did as he said. When she returned, the old man told her to boil the herb and make a tea for him to drink. She did just as he said and the old man drank the tea and then went to sleep.

The next day when he woke, he was well. He told the woman to remember carefully how she

31

gathered that herb so that she could use it for others if they suffered from the same sickness. Before the old man had shown her that herb, there had been no cure known for that sickness.

A few days passed and the old man became ill again. Once more, he was suffering from one of the sicknesses for which there was no cure. Once more, he told the woman how to go into the forest and find another herb which she must prepare for him in a certain way to cure his fever. The woman did as he said. The old man drank the medicine and he slept. The next day, his fever was gone and he was well once more.

Within a few days, however, he grew ill again. Again he gave instructions. "Go into the forest and dig a certain root. Pound it into a paste and give it to me."

Again the Bear Clan woman did as she was told and again the old man became well. So it went on many times. Each time the old man was sick and each time the medicine he prescribed for himself cured his sickness.

One morning, when the woman woke the old man was gone. In his place was a bright light, shining brighter than the sun. Within that light she thought she could see the shape of a tall man.

"I am the Creator," said the tall, shining figure. "I came to see which of my people would follow my teachings. Only you have done so, Grandchild. So I have given you and your people the gift of medicine. In front of your lodge a hemlock tree will grow.

Its branches will reach high into the air, high above all others. It will be a sign that the Bear Clan has precedence over all others and that those of the Bear Clan will be healers of the people."

Then the tall shining figure was gone. From that day on, the Bear Clan grew stronger and it was known among all the nations as the clan of the healers, those who were first given the secret of medicines by the Creator.

"I will now tell a story," said the big standing stone. Then it began to relate a tale.

The Storytelling Stone
(Seneca)

Long ago, the people had no stories to tell. It was hard for them to live without stories, especially during the long winter nights when the snow was deep outside the lodge and the people longed for something to give meaning to their lives.

"If only there were something we could listen to," the people would say. But there were no storytellers and no stories to be told.

In those days, in a certain village, there was a boy whose parents had died and whose other relatives would not care for him. This boy's name was Gahka, which means Crow. He lived by himself in a small lodge he made of branches. Among his few possessions were a bow and some arrows which his father had made for him. Because he had to take care of himself, he became a very good hunter. He also carried a small tobacco pouch which his mother had made, telling him that it was good to make an offering of some tobacco to thank the animal's spirit whenever he was successful in hunting.

The people in that village did not treat Gah-ka well. They made fun of him and laughed at his ragged clothes. Finally, one autumn, Gah-ka decided to leave the village and find a better place to live. He traveled for many days. He walked and walked until he came to a place where a large stone stood. It looked like a good place to camp. He made a fire and sat in front of it, thinking about his life and wishing that he had something to offer his people, something which would lead them to respect him. It was dark now and Gah-ka felt lonely. He leaned back against the large stone and spoke.

"If only I had something interesting to hear," he said.

"Give me tobacco and I will tell you something," a deep voice said. It sounded as if it came out of the earth itself. Gah-ka looked around and could see no one.

"What will you tell me?" Gah-ka said.

"Give me tobacco and I will tell you something," the voice repeated.

Then Gah-ka realized that the voice was coming from the great standing stone. He reached into his pouch and placed some tobacco at the base of the stone.

"Speak, Grandfather," Gah-ka said.

"I will now tell a story," said the big standing stone. Then it began to relate a tale. It was a story of the creation of the earth itself, of the woman who fell from the sky and the animals and birds who

36

helped her. Gah-ka listened to the story. It was the most wonderful thing Gah-ka had ever heard. He listened hard, trying to remember every detail. At last the story was over. Gah-ka waited and the voice spoke again.

"When a story has been told," the great stone said, "it will be the custom to give the storyteller a small gift."

Gah-ka pulled some beads from the deerskin fringe on his old, worn jacket and placed them at the base of the stone.

"Here, Grandfather. Thank you for the story."

"From now on," the great stone said, "when one announces that they will tell a story, you must say *Nyo!* And when the storyteller says *Ho!* at any time in the story, you must answer *Hey!* to show you are listening. I will now tell a story."

"Nyo!" Gah-ka said. Then the great stone began to relate a tale of the animal people and how the Bear's tail came to be short. Each time the stone said *Ho!* Gah-ka was quick to answer *Hey!* As before, Gah-ka listened closely, trying to remember every word of the story. Too soon, the story was ended and the great stone was silent. Then it spoke again.

"This is as long as my stories will go on this night."

Gah-ka was sorry to have the stories end, but he placed a few more beads at the base of the great stone.

"Thank you, Grandfather," he said. Then he went

to sleep, trying to hold every word of the stories in his mind. When he woke the next day, he wondered if he had dreamed. But the bone beads were gone and he found that he still remembered the stories. He had eaten all of his food, so he took up his bow and arrows and went hunting. As always, his luck was good and he managed to shoot several birds. As he circled back toward his camp by the big stone, he came across a village. Some of the people in the village welcomed him and asked him to sit by the fire with them. As they sat there, Gah-ka thought of the stories.

"Would you like to hear something?" he said.

"Nyo!" the people said.

"Give me some tobacco and I will tell you the story of how the Earth came to be. Each time I say *Ho!* you must answer me by saying *Hey!*"

The people did as he said. They listened closely and answered each time he said *Ho!* Before the end of his tale, everyone in the village was gathered around to listen. When the story was done, they all gave him presents. They asked him for another tale, offering him more tobacco.

"I shall tell of how the Bear lost his tail, Gah-ka said. "Do you want to hear this story?"

"Nyo!" the people said.

When Gah-ka was done, the people begged for another story.

"No," Gah-ka said. "That is the length of my stories for this evening. I must return to my lodge." Then, after promising the people he would return again the next night, Gah-ka went back to his camp by the big standing stone, carrying his presents with him. He placed tobacco on the ground and spoke.

"Grandfather, I am ready to listen again."

"I shall now tell a story," said the deep voice of the big stone.

So it went on for a long time. Each evening Gah-ka would share the stories with his new friends and each night the big standing stone would tell new stories to the boy. Sometimes people from the village would follow Gah-ka back to his camp and see him sitting in front of his fire listening, but they could hear nothing. The voice from the big stone was for Gah-ka alone to hear.

One evening, after finishing his storytelling, a girl of about Gah-ka's age approached him. She handed him a decorated pouch.

"You have many stories," she said. "Perhaps you can use this pouch in which to keep them."

Gah-ka thanked the girl and took the pouch with him. From then on, each time he learned a new story, he would put something in the pouch which would help him remember that tale. A blue jay feather reminded him of the story of how the Birds got their clothing. A small wooden Turtle reminded him of the tale of Turtle's race with Bear. As the days and weeks passed, the pouch became filled with stories.

Each time Gah-ka went to the village, he saw that girl who gave him the pouch. They became good friends and finally the girl brought him to her house. As soon as he walked through the door, the girl's mother looked up at them and smiled.

"I see that my future son-in-law has finally come through my door."

The next day, the girl came to Gah-ka's camp carrying a basket of bread. "I have brought you this because my mother agrees that we should ask you to marry me."

Gah-ka took the bread and ate it and he and the girl were married. Now the two of them lived together in his lodge near the big stone. They lived well there because Gah-ka was such a good hunter and because he had been given so many useful things by the people of the village to thank him for his stories. All through the winter he listened to stories until it was time for spring. Then the big stone spoke.

"The time for stories has ended. Now the earth is waking up and the stories must sleep. After the first frost, I will tell more stories." The next day, Gah-ka told the same thing to the people of the village.

Gah-ka and his wife spent a happy spring and summer together. They planted corn and beans and squash and took a part in the life of the village. When the first frost came, the storytelling stone began once again to share its tales of the old days with Gah-ka, who was now a young man and no longer a boy.

So it went on for a long time. Finally, one day, the

stone ended a story and was silent for a long time. Then it spoke one last time.

"Now I shall tell no more stories. I have told you all of the stories from the old time. From now on, the stories will be carried by the people, not kept in the stones. You, Gah-ka, are the first storyteller, but there will be many storytellers after you. Wherever they go, they will always be welcomed."

And from that time on, that is the way it has been.

Now Raccoon ran in front of the big stone. "You see, Grandfather," he shouted, "I am faster than you!"

Raccoon and
The Big Standing Stone
(St. Francis/Sokoki)

Once long ago Raccoon was out walking around. As usual, he was looking for something to do and, because Raccoon always likes to meddle with things, he was also looking for trouble. Before long, he came to the bottom of a very big hill. When he looked up, he thought he could see someone standing on that hilltop.

"Who is that up there?" Raccoon said. "They probably are in need of company." So Raccoon began to climb. It took him quite a while to reach the top and by the time he got up there he was feeling very proud of himself for climbing so high. He wanted to boast, but he saw no one else around. Then he noticed the big rock balanced on top of that hill. That rock was what he had seen on the hilltop.

"Grandfather," Raccoon said to the big stone, "do you see how I have climbed all the way up this mountain. Is it not wonderful?"

The rock, of course, said nothing.

"I see, Grandfather," Raccoon said, "you are so impressed you cannot speak. Do you wish you could travel around the way I do?"

Again, the rock said nothing.

"You would like to travel around as I do, wouldn't you?"

Once more, the rock did not speak.

"Grandfather," Raccoon said, "If you would like to travel as I do, just say nothing."

And the big rock said nothing.

"Good," Raccoon said. "Then I will help you travel." Raccoon began to push against the big standing stone. He pushed and pushed, but he could not move the stone. Then he looked around and found a stick. "Grandfather," he said, "this will help you travel." He put the stick under the big standing stone and began to jump on it. Now the stone began to rock back and forth.

Boomp, boomp! the stone rocked. Raccoon jumped harder. Boomp, boomp, boomp, boomp. And then it tipped far enough that it rolled over. WHABOOMP!

"GRANDFATHER," Raccoon shouted, "now you are going to travel!

WHABOOMP! WHABOOMP! WHABOOMP! The big stone went rolling down the hill, going faster and faster.

"Grandfather," Raccoon called, "you are traveling very fast. But I can travel as fast as you can!"

Then Raccoon began to run. Biddirip, biddirip, biddirip. He ran so fast that he did catch up with the rolling stone.

WHABOOMP! WHABOOMP! WHABOOMP! The stone kept rolling with Raccoon running right next to it.

"You see, Grandfather," Raccoon shouted, "I am as fast as you are."

But the big stone said nothing. It just kept rolling, WHABOOMP! WHABOOMP! WHABOOMP! WHABOOMP!

Now Raccoon ran in front of the big stone. "You see, Grandfather," he shouted, "I am faster than you!"

The big stone, though, said nothing. It just kept rolling, WHABOOMP! WHABOOMP! WHABOOMP! WHABOOMP!

Then Raccoon decided to show off. He began to zigzag back and forth in front of the big stone.

"You are very slow, Grandfather," Raccoon shouted and he ran back and forth in front of the big stone.

Just then, though, Raccoon caught his foot on a root and fell.

But the big stone could not stop. It rolled right over Raccoon. WHUMP! Then the big stone rolled on, leaving the raccoon flattened out.

Raccoon was so flat that he couldn't even breathe. He couldn't manage to do more than whisper in a small, small voice for help.

"Help. . .help. . .help. . ." he whispered.

Some birds flew overhead.

"Help. . .help. . .help. . ." Raccoon said. But they did not hear him and they flew by.

Some rabbits hopped past.

"Help. . .help. . .help. . ." Raccoon said, but they did not hear him either and they hopped past.

Finally, the smallest of all the creatures came past. It was a very tiny ant.

"Oh ant," Raccoon said, "help me!"

The ant stopped and looked at Raccoon.

"You ants," Azeban whispered, "come and help me."

"How can I help the Great Raccoon?" the ant said. "I am too small. All of the animals say that we ants are useless little people."

"Ah," Raccoon said, "you are small, but there are many of you. If you work together you can do great things. That is why I always have said that the ants are the greatest of all the people. Indeed, I am always praising the ants. The ants are wonderful. I am sure you can help me. If you help me I will always be your greatest friend."

After hearing that, the little ant went to get all his relatives. "Come quickly," he said, "our great friend Raccoon needs our help."

All of the ants came and they began to work. They pushed and pulled and they lifted Raccoon up off the ground. When they were done, Raccoon was able to shake his legs and walk around. They did a good job, but he was much flatter to the ground than he had been and he no longer could run as fast. To this day, in fact, when Raccoon hears a loud noise—like the rumbling of a big rolling stone, he will run up a tree just as quickly as he can.

As soon as those ants had put Raccoon back together they waited for him to praise them. However, Raccoon just looked down at them and said, "Go away, you ants. I have no time for useless little people." And he went on his way.

Those ants never forgot what Raccoon did to them. If you don't believe me, the next time you see a Raccoon that has been flattened out by the roadside, take a look and see what the ants are doing!

Before long, Otter came back up to the surface and threw some fish onto the shore.

How Rabbit Went to Dinner (Abenaki)

One day, Mateguas the Rabbit went to visit his friend Woodpecker. As soon as Rabbit arrived, Woodpecker invited him into his lodge.

"My friend, I'm glad you've come to see me," Woodpecker said. "I was just about to get my dinner. Would you like to eat with me?"

Rabbit, of course, agreed. It was no accident that he had arrived just at dinnertime.

Woodpecker, who was wearing a bright red headdress, took Mateguas to an old tree behind his lodge. "This will do," Woodpecker said. Then he ran up the side of the tree and began to peck at it with his beak. Soon he had gathered a great deal of food from the tree. He and Rabbit took the food back to his lodge where they had a big dinner.

"That was a fine meal," Rabbit said. "Tomorrow, my friend, you must come to my house to eat."

"I'm glad you have come, my friend," Mateguas said. "I was just about to go and collect the food for our dinner. Come along with me."

49

Then Rabbit tied a bone awl to his nose and went into the woods. He stopped at the first tree he came to, a small white birch. "This will do," Rabbit said. Then he tried to climb the tree. It was not easy. Rabbit's paws were not suited for tree climbing. Somehow, though, he managed to get up onto a branch and balance himself there. Then he tried to use his new beak to peck against the tree and collect food. But his beak did not work well at all. All he succeeded in doing was to make his head bleed. But when he saw the blood, Rabbit was pleased.

"Now," Rabbit said, "I have a red cap like my friend. Soon I will have plenty of food for both of us."

Just then Rabbit's foot slipped and he fell out of the tree to the ground with a loud thump. It looked as if Mateguas was dead. Woodpecker came over to Rabbit and jumped over him twice. As soon as he did this Rabbit sat up. Without saying a word, Woodpecker climbed up another tree—an old hollow maple, and began to gather food. Then he came down, gave the food to Rabbit and went home in disgust. Rabbit, though, took the food home, cooked it and ate it all himself. He felt very satisfied with himself.

Next day, Rabbit decided to go visiting again. He went down to the river where Otter had his lodge. The lodge was built right on' the riverbank and there was a fine slide next to it which led to the water.

"My friend," Otter said, "I am happy to see you.

50

Would you like to eat with me? I was just about to get my dinner."

"Of course," Rabbit agreed. It was no accident he had come just at dinnertime.

"I will now catch some fish," Otter said. Otter threw himself down on his stomach, slid down his mudslide, and went headfirst into the deep river. Before long, he came back up and threw some fish onto the shore. After the two of them had finished eating the fish, Rabbit was feeling very good.

"My friend, Otter," Rabbit said, "tomorrow you must come and eat with me."

The next day, Otter went to Rabbit's lodge.

"Hello, my friend," Rabbit said, "I was just about to get our dinner. Come along with me."

Rabbit led Otter through the woods until they came to a small stream. There Rabbit had made a sort of slide leading into the water.

"I will now catch some fish," Rabbit said in a loud voice. He threw himself down on his stomach and tried to coast down his slide as Otter had done. But Rabbit's fur was not slippery like Otter's and it stuck to the mud. He tried to push with his long back legs. Instead of sliding, he began to roll over and over and he fell into the water with a big splash. Rabbits are not good swimmers. Rabbit began to swallow water and cough. He struggled for a while on the surface and then he sank. Otter dove in and pulled Rabbit out. It looked as if Mateguas was dead, but Otter jumped up and down on his stomach twice and then Rabbit sat up. Without saying a word, Otter dove into the water. When he came up, he threw some fish onto the shore. He gave those fish to Rabbit and then, having no patience for someone who would try to do something he could not do, Otter went away. Rabbit, though, carried the fish home. He cooked them and ate them and felt very satisfied with himself.

On the next day, Rabbit decided to make another visit. This time he walked further down the stream to the place where Kingfisher had his camp.

"My friend," Kingfisher said, "I am glad you have come to see me. I am about to get my dinner. Will you eat with me?"

Rabbit, of course, agreed. "I will dive for a big fish," Kingfisher said. Kingfisher flew up to a cedar branch above the river. He sat there a few minutes and then dove into the river. When he came out, he had a big trout in his beak. Soon the fish was cooked and the two had a fine meal.

"My friend, Kingfisher," Rabbit said, "tomorrow you must come and eat with me."

Next day, Kingfisher came to Rabbit's lodge.

"I am glad to see you, friend," Rabbit said. "Let us go now and I will get our dinner."

Rabbit led Kingfisher to a little trickle of water in the woods. After his experience with the mud slide, Rabbit was not about to go into deep water. There were a few tiny minnows in the trickle of water.

"I will dive for a big fish," Rabbit said. He picked

up a sharp stick and held it between his teeth. Then he crawled out onto a branch above the trickle of water. He waited until one of the minnows was under him and then jumped in. But he missed the tiny fish and hit his head on a stone. Kingfisher pulled Rabbit out of the water and rolled him over twice. Then Rabbit sat up. Without a word, Kingfisher flew back to the river, dove in, and caught a big trout. He dropped the trout in front of Rabbit and then went home. He did not want to waste his time with someone who tried to do things he could never do. Rabbit, though, took the trout home, ate it and was very pleased.

When the next day came, Rabbit went visiting again. This time he decided to go see Bear. When he reached Bear's cave, Bear welcomed him.

"Hello, my friend," Bear said. "You have arrived just in time for dinner. Come and eat with me."

As Rabbit watched, Bear took a sharp knife and began to sing. Rabbit could not hear the words, but as he sang Bear began to cut at his paws with the knife. It seemed as if he was cutting pieces of flesh from his own paws, but Bear did not bleed and when he finished there were no marks on his paws at all.

"Now," Bear said, "we have plenty of meat for our stew."

Before long the stew was cooked. The two of them ate it all and Rabbit felt very good.

"My friend, Bear," Rabbit said, "tomorrow you

must come and have dinner with me."

The next day, just at dinner time, Bear came to Rabbit's lodge.

"Welcome, my friend," Rabbit said. "I am just about to make our stew."

Then Rabbit took out a sharp knife. He did not know the song Bear had sung, so he just sang some nonsense words. He cut at his paws with the knife. But no food appeared and as soon as he cut his paw it began to bleed. It hurt so much that Rabbit dropped his knife.

Bear hummed something under his breath and rubbed Rabbit's paws until the bleeding stopped. Then he sang his song and made pieces of meat appear as he cut at his own paws. He put them into Rabbit's stew pot and cooked a fine stew.

"Now," Bear said, "are you ready to eat?"

Rabbit, though, was feeling sick. He was too sick to eat or even answer. So Bear ate all of the stew by himself.

"That was a good meal, little friend," Bear said. "Will you invite me to eat on another day?"

Rabbit did not answer. With a rumbling laugh, Bear went away, thinking that Rabbit might have learned a lesson. If you decide to copy others, make sure it is something you can really do. Because, no matter how hard you try, you'll never be anyone else but you.

"So," said the Squirrel Chief to Frog and Woodchuck, "what do you have to say?"

The Little Squirrel and the Two Thieves
(Seneca)

Once, long ago, the Chief of all the Squirrels was out walking around. He could make himself invisible and so it was that he came unseen to the place in the forest where the Little Squirrel had his home in the base of a big pine tree.

Something was wrong. The Little Squirrel was running in and out of his hole in the pine tree. He ran around and around the tree and then back in again. "Thieves," he began to shout, "thieves! They have taken all the food I stored for the winter."

"This is not good," said the Squirrel Chief to himself. "I must listen and see what happens now."

Around and around the tree the Little Squirrel ran. "All gone," he shouted, "all gone. All my winter food is gone."

Before long his cries attracted some others. A big frog came hopping up from his place under a mossy rock by the stream. A fat woodchuck waddled out of his burrow at the edge of the nearby field.

"What has happened, my friend?" said the Frog.

"Thieves. Thieves! Someone took all of my food," cried the Little Squirrel, still running around and around and looking under every leaf and twig.

"Now who would take all your food?" asked the Woodchuck, clicking his teeth. "That is very sad." He looked over at the Frog.

"Ah-hah," said the Frog, clicking his teeth also, "It is very sad indeed. Who would steal all of those delicious hickory nuts and beech nuts and acorns?"

"Who indeed?" answered the Woodchuck. Then the two of them went back to their homes, leaving the Little Squirrel running back and forth, still looking for his lost winter stores.

The Squirrel Chief, who had watched it all from the top of a great oak tree, now shook his head. "Poor Little Squirrel. To work so hard getting ready for winter and now he must starve. That is not right. And those two who sympathized with him, Frog and Woodchuck—something about them was not right also. I think I will stay here and keep watch."

Before long the early autumn darkness settled over the forest. The Little Squirrel went back into his hole in the tree and slept, dreaming of his lost food. All around, everything was quiet and all the world seemed to be asleep.

But from his place high in the oak tree the Chief

of the Squirrels still kept watch, for he could see in the darkness. Soon he saw something moving at the edge of the clearing. It was the Frog, come up from his home near the stream. The Frog looked to his left, he looked to his right. He looked up, he looked down. Then he hopped to a bush on the other side of the clearing from the Little Squirrel's home. He crawled beneath it and when he came out again it was clear from the way his throat stuck out that his mouth was stuffed full of something. He looked around again and then hopped back towards his rock by the stream.

Still the Squirrel Chief watched. Now he could see another figure. It was crawling on its belly from the meadow towards the clearing. Inch by inch, looking to his left and to his right, looking up and looking down, the Woodchuck came towards the Little Squirrel's home. When he reached a large flat stone, not far from the bush the Frog had crawled beneath, he looked around one more time and then squeezed under it. When he came out his cheeks bulged as if they had been stuffed full of something. He looked around again and then crawled back towards his burrow.

For a long time the Squirrel Chief watched. First the Frog and then the Woodchuck went back and forth. Now and then they would pass each other in the darkness. Whenever they did so, they would click their teeth at each other.

"So," the Squirrel Chief said, "there is agreement among thieves." Finally the last trip had been made and all was quiet in the clearing. "Now," said the Chief of the Squirrels, "it is time for me to go home and rest. Tomorrow will be a busy day."

The sun had risen less than the width of one hand when the Squirrel Chief returned. With him were many other animals and they went to where the Little Squirrel sat sadly in front of his empty storehouse.

"Little Brother," said the Chief of the Squirrels, "we know of your misfortune. Today we have come to find the ones who robbed you. But where are your good friends, Frog and Woodchuck?"

"Elder Brother," said the Little Squirrel, "when they saw you and the other animals coming they left. Frog hopped as quickly as he could back to his rock by the stream. Woodchuck dove into his burrow and filled up the entrance with dirt from within."

The Squirrel Chief smiled. "A guilty conscience is often the best judge. Let me call them out." Then the Chief of the Squirrels called their names. He called them once, twice, three times. When he called them the fourth time his power was so great that they could not resist. Out from his rock hopped Frog. Out from his burrow crawled Woodchuck.

"Look into their houses and tell me what you find," said the Squirrel Chief to the Little Squirrel. The Little Squirrel did so and came back quickly.

"I have found all of my winter food," said the Little Squirrel. "All of it! I knew it is mine. The marks of my teeth are on every acorn and beechnut and hickory nut."

"So," said the Squirrel Chief to Frog and Woodchuck, "what do you have to say?"

But the two thieves did not answer. They knew that the penalty for stealing might be death. They were afraid.

"There is no doubt of your guilt," the Chief of the Squirrels said at last. "Now I must decide what shall be done. It is shameful that you stole from this little one. Woodchuck, hear me well. You have all spring and summer to eat the green plants and grow fat. Yet you would steal from a small animal who works very hard and will starve without winter food. Hear me, for this is how it will be from now on. You will always remember your guilt and whenever you see anyone you will hide in the ground. No longer will you stay awake all year. When the cold season comes you will go to sleep in your burrow and you will not waken again until you can see your shadow on the melting snow."

Then the Chief of the Squirrels turned to the Frog. "Frog," he said, "hear me well. You have been given a long sticky tongue and can catch all of the insects you want to be happy. Yet you also want to take food from this little one. Hear me, for this is how it will be. You too will remember your guilt. When you see anyone or hear a noise you will jump into the water and hide. From now on you will no longer eat hard foods of any kind for I now take away your teeth forever. You, too, will sleep all through the time of frost and snow. Only when the eyes of the ponds open again and the ice is gone will you waken."

Finally the Chief of the Squirrels turned to the Little Squirrel. "Little brother," he said, "it has been too easy for anyone to steal from you when you sleep. Hear me well, for this is how it will be from now on. No longer will you place your winter food in a hole at the base of a tree. Now you will do so in a hole far up in the treetop. Your eyes have been too small to see those who steal from you. Now we make them larger and place them so you can see to both sides. No longer will you sleep at night, but you will stay awake when thieves might come. Finally I give you this robe to wear. When you stretch it between your legs you can use it to glide quickly back to your tree whenever you see a thief."

And so it is to this day. The Flying Squirrel comes out at night from his hole high in the tree. With his wonderful robe he glides from place to place. The Woodchuck hides in his burrow and sleeps all through the winter. The Frog has no teeth and stays hidden in the mud all through the long cold time, though when spring comes you can hear him in the swamps and streams, croaking sadly about his lost teeth.

And in the old times, when the children of the Longhouse lost their baby teeth, they would go in the spring to such a place where the Frogs were lamenting. Then they would throw their teeth into the water and sing a little song like this:

61

Frog, Frog,
Here is my tooth.
Give me a new one
Strong as a Bear's.

And so it came to be that Crayfish has his eyes on the end of a stalk, and so it is with all other crayfish to this very day.

Why Crayfish Has His Eyes on a Stalk (Oneida)

Once, long ago, after many days of heavy rain there was a big flood. It swelled the waters of the stream where Crayfish lived far beyond the usual banks. Crayfish was very happy and went from place to place, finding all kinds of good things to eat where the water had risen.

"Be careful," said Minnow. "This water may go away again."

But Crayfish did not listen. He was too busy going around from here to there and eating all he could. Finally he had eaten so much that he grew sleepy.

"I shall just rest for a little while," he said. Then he crawled under a rock and fell fast asleep. While he slept the flood waters began to drain away. The hilltops appeared again and then the slopes of the hills like the heads of swimmers popping up out of a pond. More and more of the waters drained away and now the stream had gone back to its usual bed.

But, far away from the water now, Crayfish still slept on. The sun shone hotter and hotter and still he slept. Finally, late in the afternoon, Crayfish woke. He felt very stiff and dry. It was hard even to move. He tried to look around, but he could see nothing. His eyes had dried up.

"Yo hoh!," said Crayfish. "I should have listened. What can I do now?" Then, his legs creaking as he moved, he began to crawl. He had not gone far before he bumped into a tree. Then he sang this song:

> What kind of tree
> What kind of tree
> What kind of tree
> Is this before me?

And the tree answered, "I am an oak."

"Oh-oh," said the Crayfish, "I am still very far from water." Then he began to crawl again. On and on he went until he bumped into another tree. Once again he sang his song:

> What kind of tree
> What kind of tree
> What kind of tree
> Is this before me?

And the tree answered, "I am a maple."

"Oh-oh," said the Crayfish, feeling very discouraged, "I still have so far to go!" But still he kept crawling, even though his legs were stiff as dry twigs. After he had gone a long ways further he bumped into another tree. Once more he sang:

> What kind of tree
> What kind of tree
> What kind of tree
> Is this before me?

And the tree answered, "I am an alder."

"Eh-Heh!" cried Crayfish, feeling very excited now. "Then I do not have that far to go." He began to crawl faster and soon bumped into another tree. With great excitement he sang his song another time.

> What kind of tree
> What kind of tree
> What kind of tree
> Is this before me?

And the tree answered, "I am a willow."

When he heard that, Crayfish began to move as fast as he could. In only a few more steps he fell into the water. He felt it wash over his head and he strained so hard to see that, as the water moistened his eyes and softened the mud which had dried over them, his eyes shot right out of his head, each one on a long stalk. Crayfish waved them around. He could look in any direction he wanted. This was even better than before and so, though he had gone through much hardship, Crayfish felt that he had been rewarded for not giving up.

And so it came to be that Crayfish has his eyes on the end of a stalk, and so it is with all other crayfish to this very day.

"You are not very good at climbing, Turtle," the little bear said. *"I am a great climber!"* Turtle said. *"I was only practicing."*

How Turtle Got
His Long Neck
(Tuscarora)

Long ago, Turtle had a short neck. Still, even though it was short, he was always stretching it as far as he could so that he could hear what the other animals were doing.

Everyone said that Turtle was very wise. It was true that he could use his wits, as he did once when he won a race against Bear. However, Turtle was not as wise as he thought. In fact, Turtle was vain.

One day, Turtle heard something in a pine tree which grew near his pond. He crawled over to look. There, high in the tree, were some birds. They seemed to be eating something.

"You up there," Turtle called, "what are you doing in my tree?"

The birds stopped what they were doing and flew down to Turtle. "Don't you know?" the birds said. "We are eating the seeds in the pine cones. They are the best food in the world."

"Of course I know that," Turtle said; then he crawled back to his pond.

Soon after that, Turtle heard something in the tree again. He crawled over to look. There, high up in the tree, were some squirrels.

"You up there," Turtle called, "what are you doing in my tree?"

The squirrels climbed down the tree to where Turtle waited. "Don't you know?" the squirrels said. "We are eating the seeds in the pine cones. Don't you ever climb up and eat them? They're the best food in the world."

"Of course I know that," Turtle said. "I often climb up that tree. But I'm just not hungry right now. You go ahead and eat all you want. I'll climb up and get some later." Then Turtle crawled back to his pond, but he was not feeling happy.

It was not long before Turtle heard someone else up in his pine tree. He crawled out to look and saw a little bear high up in the tree, eating his pine seeds!

"You up there," Turtle called, "why are you eating all my food?"

The bear cub climbed down to where Turtle waited. "There's plenty to eat up there, Turtle," he said. "Would you like me to bring some down to you?"

"No," Turtle said. "I am a great climber and I can gather my own food."

"Are you sure?" said the little bear.

"Of course," Turtle said, taking a deep breath. "I

will climb up right now and get some of those seeds." Then Turtle crawled to the base of the tree and tried to climb up. He clawed and scratched at the tree but was only able to pull himself up a little way. Then he fell over, right onto his back with his feet swimming in the air. The little bear came and turned Turtle back onto his feet.

"You are not very good at climbing, Turtle," the little bear said.

"I am a great climber!" Turtle said. "I am only practicing." Then Turtle went back to the tree. He scraped and clawed and scratched, but he was not able to get up. No matter how many times he tried, he slid right back down again. The little bear watched without saying a word.

It seemed as if Turtle would have to swallow his pride. However, all of his scratching at the trunk of the tree made something happen. The tree began to ooze out sticky pine sap. Turtle saw how sticky that sap was and he got an idea.

"Now," Turtle said, "I have done my exercise. Now I am going to climb up and get my pine seeds." He covered his feet into the sticky pine sap. Then, just like a fly climbing up the wall of a lodge, he began to go up the tree. Step by slow step he went up and up until he was at the very top. At the bottom of the tree, the little bear watched and shook his head.

There, at the tip of the tree, at the end of a slender branch, was a big pine cone. It was just beyond Turtle's reach. He walked out onto the branch, but he still could not reach it. He leaned out further and further, trying to grasp it in his mouth. Just as he grabbed it, his feet slid off the branch and he began to fall. Down he went, head first!

Fortunately for Turtle, he landed in the soft mud at the edge of the pond. However, he landed nose first! He hit the mud so hard that his head was buried. When he tried to pull himself out, he was stuck. He pulled and pulled, but he could not get loose.

The little bear was watching and he took pity on Turtle. He grabbed on to Turtle's tail and began to pull. Turtle's neck stretched out longer and longer and then—POP!—he was free. But Turtle's neck was now three times as long as it had been before and all Turtles are like that today.

Turtle is always pulling his head into his shell because he is ashamed of having made such a fool of himself way back then. However, whenever Turtle hears something or becomes curious, he sticks that long neck of his way out of his shell. And to this day, Turtles do not eat pine seeds.

It was a huge female whale, her blue back so wide that Glooskap could easily climb on board. Soon she was swimming through the waves, heading for the mainland.

Glooskap and the Whale
(Micmac)

Long ago, Glooskap lived on an island. He came down to the shore, wanting to cross over to the mainland. He had no boat and the water was deep. So he began to sing a song:

      Podawawogan,
      Whale come and help me,
      Podawawogan,
      Help me to cross

His song had great power and soon a whale rose to the surface of the water and swam close in the deep water to the place where Glooskap stood. This whale, though, was not a big whale and Glooskap was a giant. Glooskap put one foot on the whale's back. As soon as he began to put his weight onto the whale it sank. Glooskap pulled his foot back.

"Thank you, brother," he said, "but you are not strong enough to carry me."

Then Glooskap sang his song again:

      Podawawogan,
      Whale come and help me,

Podawawogan,
Help me to cross

This time, the largest of all the whales came. It was a huge female, her blue back so wide that Glooskap could easily climb on board. Soon she was swimming through the waves, heading for the mainland.

This great whale, though, was worried about going aground. She knew that the water grew shallow close to the mainland. Glooskap, however, did not want to get his feet wet. Before long, they started to get close to shore.

"Can you see the land from my back?" the great whale said.

The land was now in sight, but Glooskap was afraid she would dive and leave him in the water if he told the truth.

"No," he said, "land is still out of sight. Swim faster, Grandmother, swim faster."

Then the whale began to swim faster. But as she swam, she looked down and she could see the shells of the clams below her. This frightened her, for she knew that meant the water was no longer so deep.

"Can you see the land from my back," she said, "doesn't it show itself like the string of a bow?"

"No," Glooskap said, "we're still far from land. Swim faster, Grandmother, swim faster."

Now the clams did not like Glooskap. He had gathered many of them and eaten them, making great mounds of empty shells on the shore. The clams began to sing:

"You are close to land,

throw him off, throw him off,
You are close to land,
throw him off, let him drown"

"What are the clams singing?" the great whale said. She could not understand their language.

"Ah," Glooskap said, "I can understand them. They are saying to hurry, to hurry along. To hurry along for we're still far from shore."

"Then I must hurry," the whale said. She dove with her mighty tail—and found herself grounded up on the beach! She was stuck and could not get free.

Glooskap climbed from her back.

"Grandchild," the great whale said, "you have been my death. I will never swim in the sea again."

Glooskap shook his head. "No, Grandmother," he said. "I will not let you suffer. You will swim in the sea again." He pulled his great bow from his back and pushed with it against the great whale's head. He pushed her from the beach and back into the deep water again.

The whale was very happy. She leaped and danced in the waves, throwing great mountains of spray up as she breached. To this day the great whales dance that way, remembering how Glooskap pushed their grandmother back into the water. Then the whale turned back towards Glooskap.

"Grandchild," she said, "can you give me something?"

Glooskap took his pipe from his pouch. "I will

give you this, Grandmother," he said.

The great whale took the pipe. To this day you may see the big whales blowing the smoke up into the air from that pipe which Glooskap gave their grandmother when she helped him come to the mainland.

Glooskap picked the boat up and looked it over very carefully. He looked at the small people on the boat. They
had hair on their faces, just like a bear, but they seemed
to be human beings.

Glooskap Visits the King
(Penobscot)

One day, as Glooskap was walking around, he saw a strange looking boat far out to sea. It seemed to have trees with big white leaves growing out of it and it was bigger than any canoe.

"I've never seen a boat like that," he said. "I need to take a closer look."

He took a deep breath and he started to grow larger and larger. When he was large enough, he waded out into the ocean until he came to the boat. He picked it up and looked it over very carefully. He looked at the small people on the boat. They had hair on their faces, just like a bear, but they seemed to be human beings. It was hard to understand their language at first. Glooskap, though, could speak to all of the people and all of the animals and finally he figured out what they were saying.

One of the hairy-faced men with a big hat was shouting at him, "You must put us down! This ship belongs to the King."

"Where does this King live?" Glooskap said.

"He lives across the ocean," the little man said. "He is the mightiest person on earth. You must put us down or he will be very angry at you."

"Is that so?" Glooskap said. "Then I had better put you down and send you back to your King."

Glooskap put the boat back down in the water. He took a deep breath and then blew so hard that the boat shot across the waves and was soon out of sight.

Glooskap went straight to his Grandmother Woodchuck's lodge.

"Grandmother," he said, "let us go across the ocean and see this King that the new people talk about."

"Let us go then, Grandmother Woodchuck answered.

Glooskap and Grandmother Woodchuck stepped onto the island. Immediately, that island became a giant ship, just like the one Glooskap had looked at before. The pine trees in the center of the island became the masts. The squirrels on the island became the sailors and began running up and down the mast. Then Glooskap set sail across the ocean for the land of the King.

When they reached the King's land, it was just getting dark. They anchored the ship just off the coast and it turned back into an island. Then Glooskap and his Grandmother Woodchuck went to sleep.

The King's castle was close to the coast and when he woke in the morning, he saw that island and all of the tall trees.

"What is this?" the King said. "Why have I never noticed that island before? Those tall trees will make fine timber. I must send my men over to cut those trees down."

As soon as the King's men arrived on the island, they began to cut the trees. Some of the men saw the squirrels and began to shoot at them. That woke Glooskap and his Grandmother up.

"What is happening, Grandmother?" Glooskap said.

"Some men are cutting down our trees and trying to kill our squirrels," Grandmother Woodchuck said.

Glooskap stood up. "What are you doing to my trees?" he said to the men.

"These trees belong to the King. He sent us to cut them down."

Glooskap became angry. "Grandmother," he said, "shall I throw these men into the sea?"

"No, Glooskap," Grandmother Woodchuck said, "we have come to visit here. That would not be polite. Just send them home to their King."

So Glooskap began to pick up the men. He took their axes and guns away from them and put the men into their boat.

"Go tell your King that Glooskap and his Grandmother have come to see him," Glooskap said. Then he pushed the boat with his hand. He just gave it a gentle push, but the boat shot across the water so fast that when it reached the shore it slid all the way up to the door of the castle.

The King looked out and saw his men. "What are you doing here?" he said. "Why are you not cutting those trees?"

"Your Majesty," the captain of the men said, "someone on that island wouldn't let us cut the trees. He said that he and his Grandmother have come to visit you."

The King grew very angry. He called to a group of his soldiers. "Bring those people to me," he said.

The soldiers went to the island and found Glooskap and his grandmother.

"Are you the ones who have come to visit the King?" they said.

Glooskap was pleased. "You see, Grandmother, they have come to bring us to see the King. We must go with them."

When they came in front of the King, he stared at them.

"Who are you?" he said.

"I am Glooskap and this is Grandmother Woodchuck. Who are you?"

"No one can ask the King who he is," the King said.

"But I have just asked you," Glooskap said.

The King was very angry now. "Why did you stop my men when they went to cut my trees?" he said.

"That island is my ship," Glooskap said.

"If you will not answer my questions, you will have to die," the King said. Then he ordered his men to shoot Glooskap. Glooskap pulled out his stone pipe and began to puff on it. The soldiers fired their guns at him, but the bullets just bounced off him.

"Stab him with your bayonets."

The soldiers charged at Glooskap with their bayonets. He stood there smoking his pipe and smiling. The bayonets broke against his skin.

Now the King was very angry. "Put him and his Grandmother into the biggest cannon and shoot it!" he said.

Glooskap and his Grandmother let the soldiers pick them up and carry them to the biggest cannon. The soldiers loaded in the gunpowder, put Glooskap and his Grandmother into the cannon, and shoved in the wadding.

"All is ready, your Majesty," said the captain.

"Fire the cannon!" the King said.

The captain touched a match to the cannon. There was a great explosion and the air was filled with smoke. When it cleared away, Glooskap and his Grandmother stood there unharmed, smoking their stone pipes. The great cannon lay all in pieces at their feet.

Glooskap looked at Grandmother Woodchuck.

"These people are very rude," he said. "They do not know the right way to treat a visitor."

"It is time for us to go home," Grandmother Woodchuck said.

They walked down to the water and stepped back onto their island. It turned back into a ship and sailed away towards the west while the King and his men stared in disbelief.

When they got back home, they turned their ship back into an island again. You can still see it just off the shore. Sometimes you can see the smoke from Glooskap's pipe rising above that island—though some think it is only fog. Some old people say that Glooskap and his Grandmother have their wigwam there on that island and they are making arrowheads. They take a long time with each arrowhead to make sure it is just right. When their lodge is filled with those arrowheads, Glooskap will come out and help the Indian people get back the land that the King and his men stole from them.

The ducks came inside and formed a circle. The music was good and they began to dance while Nanabush instructed them what to do.

Nanabush and the Ducks
(Anishinabe)

One day, Nanabush was out walking around. He had been walking for a long time and he was feeling hungry. As he walked along, he came to a big pond. Out on the water he could see some ducks. The longer he looked at them, the hungrier he felt. But those ducks were far out on the water and he knew that if he tried to swim out to them, they would fly away. Not only that, the water was cold.

"Hmmm," Nanabush said, "I think there should be a dance. Yes, I will have a special dance and invite my friends, the ducks."

Then Nanabush went back to his lodge and got ready. He built a fire in the center of the lodge and brought out his drum. He began to beat on the drum and sing.

> Way hey hey hey, all you ducks come
> Way hey hey hey, come and dance
> Way hey hey hey, all you ducks come,
> Way hey hey hey, come and dance.

The sound of his drumming and singing reached

the ducks as they swam around out on the pond.

"Ahn-hahan," the ducks said. "Nanabush is having a special dance for us. We must go to his lodge."

So the ducks began to flock to Nanabush's lodge. The wood ducks and the teal, the golden-eyes and the buffleheads, the canvasbacks and the mallards, the black ducks and the fish ducks, all of them came to the lodge where Nanabush was singing and drumming.

Way hey hey hey, all you ducks come
Way hey hey hey, come and dance
Way hey hey hey, all you ducks come,
Way hey hey hey, come and dance.

They looked inside, and Nanabush, who sat near the door of the lodge, motioned them in with his head as he drummed and sang:

Way hey hey hey, all you ducks come
Way hey hey hey, come and dance
Way hey hey hey, all you ducks come,
Way hey hey hey, come and dance.

The ducks came inside and formed a circle. The music was good and they began to dance and dance, while Nanabush instructed them what to do with his singing:

Way hey hey hey, close your eyes now
Way hey hey or they'll turn red
Way hey hey hey, dance with eyes closed
Way hey hey against the smoke.

It *was* very smoky inside the lodge and none of them wanted to have red eyes. So all of the ducks closed their eyes as they danced around. They were dancing and dancing. Among the ducks was one big long-legged stork who had come along to the dance with all the others. As he danced, he stepped close to Nanabush. Nanabush reached out and grabbed him by the neck with one hand. Then Nanabush whispered in the stork's ear, "If you want to keep breathing, keep your eyes closed and take this drum!"

The stork took the drum, freeing Nanabush's hands. He beat the drum while Nanabush continued to sing:

Way hey hey hey, keep your eyes closed
Way hey hey or they'll get red
Way hey hey hey, keep your eyes closed
Way hey hey or they'll get red.

Then Nanabush started to reach out and grab the ducks as they passed by him. As he grabbed each duck he would twist its neck and sing even louder to cover the sound of its squawking. But just as the coot got close, it opened its eyes and saw what Nanabush was doing.

"Fly for your lives!" the coot shouted. "Nanabush is killing us."

The wood duck opened its eyes to see and its eyes became red. But the coot was right and the wood duck flew for the door of the lodge, followed by all of the other ducks. Nanabush kicked at the coot as it flew by him. His foot hit the coot in its backside. Ever since then the coot's legs have been way back near the end of its body and, because it opened its eyes as did the wood duck, the eyes of the coot are red.

The ducks flew so fast as they escaped from Nanabush's lodge that they knocked the lodge to pieces and knocked Nanabush down. It was good that they escaped or there might have been no ducks left in the world today, for Nanabush would have gotten all of them if he could.

When the ducks were gone, Nanabush stood up. He was still feeling pleased with himself, for he had twisted the necks of enough ducks to make a good meal for himself. He decided to cook them in the old way. He coated the ducks with mud and then buried them in the embers of his fire and waited for them to cook. As he sat there, though, he heard a squeaking noise. That noise bothered him.

Sqwwweee, sqweeee

sqweeeee, sqweeee

"Who is making that squeak?" Nanabush said.

Sqwwweee, sqweeee

sqweeeee, sqweeee

Nanabush looked around, trying to find out who was bothering him. Then he looked up and saw what it was. The branches of two trees above his head were rubbing together as the trees moved in the wind.

"Tree squeak," Nanabush said, "be quiet. You are bothering me."

Sqwwweee, sqweeee

sqweeeee, sqweeee

"If you don't stop," Nanabush said, "I will climb up and make you stop!"

Sqwwweee, sqweeee
sqweeeee, sqweeee

That made Nanabush very angry. He climbed up into the tree. When he came to the two branches which were rubbing together in the wind, he began to push them apart so that the sound would stop. He pulled with one hand and pushed with the other. He put his back against one branch and his feet against the other and he shoved. Just then, a gust of wind swept through the trees. It knocked Nanabush off balance. The two tree limbs snapped back together and trapped Nanabush in between them in such a way that he couldn't get out.

"Let go of me!" said Nanabush, but the tree limbs did not move.

Nanabush looked around. He could see his cooking pit down below. He could smell the delicious odor of the ducks cooking. That made Nanabush feel very hungry indeed. He struggled harder to get free, but the tree branches would not move.

"Well," Nanabush said, "I can keep guard up here. I can see very far in every direction. I can make sure no one comes and steals my dinner before I can eat it."

Then Nanabush began to look around. He looked north and east, south and west. There, over the hill to the west, he could see a wolf. The wolf was headed away from him.

"HEY," Nanabush shouted, "HEY!"

The wolf heard Nanabush and turned to look up in the tree.

"DON'T COME THIS WAY," Nanabush shouted. "IF YOU COME THIS WAY YOU WON'T FIND ANYTHING GOOD TO EAT! YOU WON'T FIND ANY DUCKS BEING COOKED!"

That made the wolf curious. He started to come closer and then he smelled the ducks cooking in the coals. He went right to the fire pit, even though Nanabush kept shouting at him.

"GO AWAY, THERE IS NOTHING THERE TO EAT. THERE AREN'T ANY DUCKS COOKING IN THOSE COALS!"

The wolf began to dig the ducks out of the coals. He ate until he could eat no more. Then he looked up at Nanabush in the tree, nodded to him, and went away.

Nanabush stayed stuck in that tree for a long time. Finally, a gust of wind came through the trees again. It blew the two branches apart and Nanabush fell to the ground. His ducks had been eaten and he was still hungry, so once again he started walking around. And that is as far as this story of Nanabush will walk with him today.

He reached into his pouch for a stone and found the little turtle. He pulled it out, drew back his arm, and
threw! The turtle struck the water just right and started to skip.

Skunny Wundy's Skipping Stone (Seneca)

Long ago, in a little village by the Otsiningo River, there lived a boy named Skunny-Wundy. He was not as big or as strong as the other boys, but he could do two things better than the others—think fast and skip stones. Though the other boys tried, none beat him at stone skipping. Sometimes they'd ask Skunny-Wundy to join them throwing stones at frogs and turtles on the river bank. Skunny-Wundy would never do that. His mother had told him stories about the animals and he didn't want to hurt them. Finally, none of the other boys would skip stones with him, but Skunny-Wundy didn't mind. Almost any day he could be found by the river, skipping stones. Skunny-Wundy always went to the south because of what his parents told him.

"Why must I never go to the north?" Skunny-Wundy asked.

"Listen," his mother said. "To the north there are

terrible beings, giants whose skins are made of stone. Arrows and spears bounce off them. They are taller than pine trees! And do you know what they like to eat?"

Skunny-Wundy shook his head, though he knew the answer. He'd heard such stories from his parents before.

"People!" said Skunny-Wundy's father. "A boy like you would be one bite for a Stone Giant. But if they don't see people, they forget we exist. If they weren't so stupid they would have wiped out all the people long ago. So do not go to the north."

For a long time, or so it seemed to Skunny-Wundy, he did as his parents said. Whenever he skipped stones on the river he went south. When he returned he never went past his own village. But it grew harder and harder to find good skipping stones.

One day Skunny-Wundy rose very early, before the sun. No one else was awake. He said to himself, "It won't matter if I walk just a *little* ways towards the north. I won't go far."

As soon as he started north he found a good skipping stone. Another one, though, further on, was better! Gradually, he went around the bend in the river, leaving the village far behind. Finally, as the sun reached the middle of the sky, he found a stone that was perfect. It was just the right weight, smooth and flat. Setting his feet, he cocked his arm and threw. It skipped twelve times before it sank, leaving a row of rings on the river's smooth surface.

"WEH-YOH!" Skunny-Wundy shouted. "I am the best skipper of stones in the world!"

"HAH-A-AH," roared a great voice over his head, so loud it shook the ground under his feet. "YOU ARE NOT THE GREATEST SKIPPER OF STONES!"

Skunny-Wundy looked up. There, looming over the trees, was the biggest, hungriest-looking Stone Giant anyone could imagine. It reached down, picked up a flat stone as big as a bear and threw it across the river. That stone skipped fifteen times before it sank!

"HAH-A-AH," the Stone Giant roared again. "YOU SEE WHO IS THE GREATEST SKIPPER OF STONES. NOW I AM GOING TO EAT YOU."

Skunny-Wundy knew it would do no good to run. The Stone Giant would catch him in one stride. But he could use his wits.

"Hunh!" Skunny-Wundy said. "Are you afraid I will beat you?"

"ENHH?" said the Stone Giant. "I AM AFRAID OF NO ONE." He stomped his foot on the ground so hard it almost knocked Skunny-Wundy off his feet.

"If you are not afraid," Skunny-Wundy said, "we will have a contest to see who's better at skipping stones."

"NYOH!" the Stone Giant said. "I AGREE. GO AHEAD. THROW YOUR STONE. TRY TO BEAT ME."

"Ah," Skunny-Wundy said, "my arm is too tired

now. I've been skipping stones all day. Let me go home and rest. I promise I'll come back tomorrow for our contest."

"NYOH," the Stone Giant said. "THAT IS GOOD. TOMORROW WHEN THE SUN IS AT THE TOP OF THE SKY WE WILL SKIP STONES. IF I WIN, THEN I WILL EAT YOU. IF YOU WIN, THEN MAYBE I WILL NOT EAT YOU."

"I agree," said Skunny-Wundy, walking backwards as he spoke. "I will return tomorrow."

Skunny-Wundy walked very slowly until he was around the bend in the river and the Stone Giant could no longer see him. Then he ran as fast as he could. He didn't stop until he was within sight of his village. He sat down on a log and began to laugh. It had been so easy to outwit the Stone Giant. It was as his father told him. Stone Giants were stupid. Then Skunny-Wundy remembered. He'd given his word he would return the next day! His parents had always told him breaking a promise was a terrible thing. Not only that, if he didn't keep his word, the Stone Giant might come looking for him. It only had to follow the river. It wouldn't just find Skunny-Wundy, but his whole village. It wouldn't just eat him, it would eat everyone.

When Skunny-Wundy went to bed that night he was very quiet. His mother asked if anything was wrong, but Skunny-Wundy said nothing. If he told his parents, they'd try to fight the monster. It would eat them, too. The next morning, before sunrise, Skunny-Wundy walked slowly towards the north along the river, certain that this would be his last day. As he walked, though, he kept looking down. Perhaps if he found just the right stone he'd be able to beat the Stone Giant. He kept picking up stones and dropping them. None were just right. Then he heard a little voice from the ground ahead of him. It was calling his name!

"Skunny-Wundy, Skunny-Wundy. Take me, Skunny-Wundy. Take me, take me, take me."

Skunny-Wundy looked down among the flat stones. Was one of them talking to him? Then he saw that what he thought to be a stone was a little turtle, its head sticking out of its shell.

"Skunny-Wundy," the turtle said again, "take me, take me, take me, take me."

"You want me to use you as a skipping stone?"

"Nyoh, nyoh, nyoh, nyoh!" said the little turtle. "We can win, we can win, we can win, we can win!"

"All right," Skunny-Wundy said. "A small friend is better than no friend at all when you're in trouble."

The little turtle pulled in its head and legs. It looked just like a skipping stone. Then Skunny-Wundy placed the turtle into his belt pouch and continued on. The sun was high in the sky now. Soon he would soon reach the place where he was to meet the Stone Giant. He could hear a sound like thunder rolling and lightning striking. Skunny-Wundy peeked around a bend in the river. There stood the Stone Giant, holding a huge boulder. "HHRRUUMMM," the stone giant rumbled, making a sound like thunder. Then it hurled the stone. The stone skipped sixteen times and hit the other side with a sound like lightning. CRACK! Skunny-Wundy thought about running away, but he remembered his promise. He stepped around the bend.

"KWEH!" rumbled the Stone Giant as it saw him. "LITTLE FOOD, I HAVE BEEN WAITING FOR YOU. ARE YOU READY TO BE EATEN?"

Skunny-Wundy held up his hand. "Wait!" he said. "First we must have our contest. Remember?"

"HAH-A-AH!" the Stone Giant laughed. "THROW YOUR STONE. THEN I SHALL BEAT YOU AND THEN I SHALL EAT YOU."

"No," Skunny-Wundy said, "you must go first. You challenged me."

"NYOH," the Stone Giant said. "THAT IS GOOD." It picked up a stone large as a lodge and then, "HHRRUMMM," hurled it. It struck the water with a great whap! each time it skipped. It skipped seventeen times and knocked down a dozen trees on the other side.

"NOW, LITTLE FOOD," the Stone Giant said, reaching for Skunny-Wundy.

"First I must throw my stone," Skunny-Wundy said, his voice was calm, but his heart was beating so fast he thought it would burst. He reached into his pouch for a stone and found the little turtle. He pulled it out, drew back his arm, and threw! The turtle struck the water just right and started to skip. One, two, three, four, five six, seven times it skipped.

Eight, nine, ten, eleven, twelve times, but it was slowing down. Just then, the little turtle stuck out its legs and began kicking. Thirteen, fourteen, fifteen times it skipped. Sixteen, seventeen, eighteen, nineteen, twenty times and now it was skipping in circles. Twenty-one, twenty-two, twenty-three, twenty-four times it skipped and then sank beneath the surface.

"Weh-yoh!" Skunny-Wundy shouted. "I have won. Eat me if you want, but you have lost!"

The Stone Giant became very angry. It had never been defeated at anything before. It started to shake with rage. It shook and shook. It shook so hard cracks appeared in its body. Flakes of rock flecked from its cheeks. Harder and harder it shook until it collapsed into a pile of little stones.

So it was that with the help of his friend, the little turtle, Skunny-Wundy defeated his first stone giant.

"Weyhey!" Big Duck shouted, "I can fly with the birds. My power is very great."

The Man Who was Friends with Trickster (Seneca)

Once there was a man named Big Duck. Big Duck was very lazy. When all the other men were out hunting, or there was work to be done, he would always find an excuse to get out of it.

"My husband," his wife said one day, "all you ever do is sit around and daydream. There is hardly any food in our house and what there is, you are putting into your big stomach. Go and see if you can do something useful."

So Big Duck got up from his bed, limped carefully to the door and went outside. As soon as he was out of sight of his house, he began to walk normally.

"Ah," he said, "if only I had a good friend to visit, one who has plenty of food in his house and doesn't expect a poor sick man to work."

Before long, Big Duck came to the place in the woods where he often went to rest when his wife could no longer stand his laziness. There was a bed of soft moss under a big tree and it was a very good place to sleep. No one ever disturbed him here, for it was deep in the woods. He sat down and almost immediately fell asleep. It seemed he had been asleep only a short time when he woke up, but there, close by, he saw something strange. It was a bark lodge.

"Eh-heh!" he said, "what a fine house. Why have I never seen this lodge before? I must take a closer look."

Coming closer, he saw the lodge was a very big one, indeed. There was the head of the clan animal carved in wood and hung over the door. But Big Duck could not tell what kind of animal it was. It looked like no animal he had ever seen before. Just then a strange man came out of the lodge.

"My friend," the man said, "I am glad to see you. I thought that you would come to visit me sooner or later. Come inside and we shall eat."

Big Duck never refused an invitation to eat. He went quickly into the lodge before his new friend could change his mind.

"Now then," said the strange man, "I will make some fine corn soup for you." He lifted a pot down from the rack above his bed. Then he took another pot which was filled with rotten fish. The smell was so strong that Big Duck had to step back. But he was curious to see what would happen next.

"Onenhsto!" the strange man said and clapped his hands.

Immediately the pot was filled with hot corn soup. Then he and Big Duck sat down and ate. They ate until they were both so full they could eat no more.

"Niaweh," said Big Duck. "I thank you very much my friend. Can I borrow a pot and take some of this delicious soup home with me?"

His new friend smiled. "Why carry home this old soup?" he said. "I will teach you how to make corn soup this way yourself. All you have to do is take this empty pot and put anything rotten into it. Then you only have to say *Onenhsto!* and your pot will be filled with soup."

So Big Duck set out for home, carrying the pot. Somehow, though, the way home seemed to take much longer than he remembered. It had been easy to come to the place in the forest where his friend had his lodge, but it was a long walk to get back home. He sat down to rest on a log and realized that he had been walking so long that he was hungry again. He looked around and found some rotten wood. Placing it into the pot he called out the magic word, "Onenhsto!" and clapped his hand. Immediately the pot was full of steaming corn soup. Big Duck ate it all up. Then, after resting for a while, he continued home.

When he arrived at the lodge, his wife was waiting.

"Where have you been, Lazy One?" she said. "All of the other men have brought home food. Will we have to go hungry again because you spent the day sleeping in the woods?"

"Hah!" Big Duck said. "I have brought home food also. With my magic pot we will have corn soup any time we want. Bring the children into the lodge and I will show you how my good friend taught me to make food."

As soon as everyone was seated, Big Duck took out his magic pot. He placed some spoiled meat—which smelled so bad even the dogs would not touch it—into the pot.

"*Onenhsto!*" he shouted, clapping his hands. Immediately the pot began to overflow with an awful-smelling mess.

"You see," Big Duck said, dancing around, "You see how I can make good food?"

But his wife and children did not answer, for they had been driven out of the lodge by the awful smell. It was only when his wife came back with a pot full of water and threw it into the lodge that Big Duck came to his senses and stopped dancing around.

"Your friend is a troublemaker," Big Duck's wife said. "He has made you think that rotten meat is corn soup. Now you must clean up our lodge and learn to provide for us the right way as the other men do."

Big Duck felt very sad. Why had his friend tricked him this way? As soon as he had cleaned up the mess, he decided to go back to the lodge in the woods and find out. He set out on the trail and came to his friend's lodge in no time at all.

"My friend," said the strange man, standing up

to take Big Duck by the hand, "I have been wait-ing for you to come and see me again. Did your fam-ily enjoy the meal you made for them?"

"No," Big Duck said, "when I placed rotten meat into the pot and spoke the word, the pot overflowed with an awful-smelling mess. My wife made me clean it up and then drove me from the lodge."

"I cannot understand how this happened," said the friend. "Did you do as I told you and not use the magic pot until you were at home with your family?"

Big Duck said nothing, but he looked very unhappy.

"My friend," the strange man said, "come and sit with me. We will have another meal together. Let me get my war club."

Then, placing his war club on a bench, he picked up a heavy stick. He put his foot on top of the war club and said, "Pumpkins, you are hidden in my war club. Pumpkins come out!" Then he struck the head of his war club with the heavy stick. As soon as he did so, a fat pumpkin came rolling out.

Big Duck was delighted. This was even better than making corn soup. His friend cooked the pumpkin and the two of them ate it.

"Now," the friend said, "I will give you the same power. Strike your war club against mine. If you hit it, you will have the power to make pumpkins roll forth."

Big Duck took his war club and struck it against his friend's. WHACK!

"Now," said the friend, "all you have to do is say *Pumpkins Come Out!* and strike your club with a stick and you will have plenty to eat. Remember, though, you must wait until you get home to do this."

"Niaweh," said Big Duck, who was already half-way out the door. "I can't wait to show my wife how I can make pumpkins!"

Once again, though the way to his friend's house seemed short, the way home seemed very long. Feeling tired, Big Duck sat down on a log and placed his war club on the ground. Then, picking up a stick, he said, "I wonder what would happen if I should strike my war club like this—WHACK!— and say *Pumpkins Come Out!*"

As soon as he did so, a fat pumpkin rolled out of the head of his war club. Big Duck was pleased to see how strong his magic was. He made a fire right there, baked the pumpkin, and ate it. Then, putting his magic club on his shoulder, he continued home.

"Wife!" he called when he reached his village. "Come and see. I have great powers now. I shall make pumpkins appear for the whole village."

Not only Big Duck's wife, but most of the other people in the village came and gathered round. Then Big Duck placed his war club on the ground. He picked up a heavy stick, swung it high above his head and brought it down with all of his force. But instead of hitting his war club, he struck his own big toe and fell to the ground in pain.

"Oh!" he cried, "Oh! My toe is broken."

Shaking her head, Big Duck's wife helped him limp to his lodge. "My husband," she said, "Who is teaching you these crazy things? That new friend of yours must be Sojy, the Trickster himself. Promise me you will stop doing such foolish things."

However, as Big Duck lay in his bed, he remembered what his friend said about waiting until he got home. "That was it," he said to himself. "Next time I will do exactly what my friend tells me to do. Then I will show my wife I can provide food magically without having to work for it."

Within a few days, Big Duck's toe was well enough so that he could walk. He waited until his wife had gone to the lodge of one of the other women. Then he quickly walked out of the village, heading for his friend's lodge in the woods. However, just as he was crossing the stream below the village, he saw a familiar person standing on the other side with a sharp knife in his hand.

"Niaweh skanoh!" Big Duck said. "Is that you, my friend?"

"It is indeed," the strange man said. "I have not seen you for some time. Have you been ill?"

"Ah . . ." Big Duck said. "I have been busy. But tell me, my friend, is your name Sojy?"

"So I have been called," his friend said. "And I do have many tricks. I will now show you a good one you can use to catch fish."

Then, taking his sharp knife, Sojy, The Trickster, began to whittle at his own shins. Instead of bleed-

106

ing, his shins became as sharp as the knife itself.

"Watch," Sojy said, "I will get some fish." He waded into the stream and began to kick with his legs underwater. Each time he kicked he struck a fish and it floated to the top of the water. When there were many fish floating on top of the stream he climbed out on the back, spat into his hands and rubbed his legs. As soon as he did so, his legs were healed back to normal.

"Now," Sojy said, "shall we eat some fish?"

Big Duck loved to eat fish. He helped his friend gather them from the stream. Soon they had made a fire, cooked the fish, and eaten them all.

"That is a good trick," Big Duck said. "Are you sure I can do it?"

"Of course," said Sojy. "Did not the other tricks I taught you work? Just remember that you will only have enough power to do this trick one time."

Then Sojy spat into his hands and rubbed his hands on Big Duck's legs.

Soon Big Duck was walking back along the stream towards his village. But, as he walked, he saw there were many fat fish in the pools. "What was it my friend told me?" he said. "Oh yes, he said I can only do this trick once to show the people. But if I were to wade in and catch just a few fish now, that surely would not count, would it?"

Then Big Duck pulled out his knife and cut away at his shins. Just as Sojy had told him it would, the trick worked and his shins became as sharp as the knife blade. He waded into the water kicking about and soon fat fish were floating on the surface. Big Duck gathered them up, made a fire, and ate every one. After resting a while he sighed.

"Ah," he said, "It is good to be a man with so much power. Now I must go show my wife my new trick."

As soon as he reached the village, Big Duck began to shout.

"Everyone, come with me! I am going to show you a trick I have learned. I am the only one with enough power to do this. I shall catch many fish and we will all have a big feast."

Big Duck's wife was one of the first people to come out of her lodge.

"My husband," she said. "Listen to me before it is too late. I have seen you do this sort of thing before."

Big Duck, though, would not listen. He led the villagers to the stream, sat down on the bank and pulled out his knife.

"Now," he said, "I will work my trick." He began to cut at his shins. But as soon as he did so, blood flowed out. It hurt so much that he fainted.

When he came to he was back in his lodge with bandages on his legs.

"Now," said his wife, "have you finally learned your lesson? If you don't stop doing the things Trickster shows you, you are going to kill yourself."

Although it took him some time to heal, Big Duck could not stop thinking about Trickster.

"Surely," Big Duck said to himself, "my friend

has more things he can teach me. This time I will be sure to do just what he tells me. Then I will show my wife!"

As soon as Big Duck felt well enough to walk, he went right into the woods, heading for the strange man's lodge. On his way, however, he passed by a pond. There was his friend, sitting by the edge of the pond and making string out of basswood bark.

"Where have you been?" said Sojy. "I have missed you. Did you catch plenty of fish with the trick I taught you? Are those bandages wrapped around your legs?"

"I did very well," Big Duck said, "very well, indeed. But I . . . ah, slipped when I was carrying all of the fish back to the village and scraped my shins. That is why I have the bandages."

"That is good," said Sojy. "I would hate to think you hurt yourself by doing that trick in the wrong way. Now, however, you are here and just in time to catch some ducks. Look out there on the pond."

Big Duck looked. There, far out in the middle of the pond, was a flock of ducks floating on the water. They were too far away for a hunter with a bow to strike them. "Watch," said Sojy. He dove into the water and did not come up. Soon, the ducks in the middle of the lake began to vanish one by one. Before long, Sojy's head popped up again near the shore. All of the ducks were tied by their legs to his magical cords.

"Now," said Sojy, "we will have our feast." They made a fire pit, packed clay from the bank of the pond around the ducks and baked them in the coals. Big Duck ate until he could hardly stand up.

"This is the best trick of all," he said. "Can I do it also?"

"My friend," said Sojy, "take these cords. Now you can catch ducks."

"How many times can I do this trick?" said Big Duck. This time he was not going to make any mistakes.

"You may do this as often as you wish, as long as you are not greedy," Sojy said, smiling as he did so.

Big Duck began to walk back home, but as he walked he noticed another flock of ducks at the far end of the pond.

"Since there is no harm in doing my trick as often as I want," he said, "I should try out my power." Then, holding the cords in his hand, he jumped in and swam underwater to the flock of ducks. In no time at all he had fastened all of them to his cords and brought them out on shore.

"Wey-hey!" he said. "This is the best trick of all. I will bring these to my wife and show her what a powerful man her husband truly is."

However, as Big Duck spoke, a flock of geese came winging in and landed in the middle of the pond.

"Hay!" Big Duck said. "If I bring these home, my wife will never call me foolish again. He unfastened his cords from the ducks and jumped back into the water. In no time at all he was underneath the geese and he began fastening the cords to their legs.

There were many geese and it took him longer than he had expected. Finally, all of the geese were fastened to his magical cords. Then he began to yank on the cords, trying to pull the geese underwater. The geese, though, were too strong. Big Duck wrapped the cord tightly around his wrists and pulled again. This time, the geese became alarmed. With a great flurry of wings, they rose out of the water, carrying Big Duck with them! Soon he was high over the trees.

"Wey-hey!" Big Duck shouted. "I can fly with the birds. My power is very great." However, as the flock of geese swooped low near Big Duck's village, the wet cords began to slip from his grasp. He tried to hold onto them, but it was no use. The last of them slipped free and Big Duck began to fall. Down he fell, down, down, and landed—Whoosh!—right in a hollow tree with a broken top. He was not hurt, but when he tried to move he found he was stuck. As he moved his head, he saw a knothole right in front of his eyes. He leaned closer and he could see outside. He was near the stream where the women came to bathe. Just then, some of the young women from the village came to the stream.

"Ah-hah!" Big Duck said. He spoke so loudly that one of the young women heard him.

"What is that?" she said. "I heard a strange voice."

"I am here inside the tree," Big Duck said. "I am a magical bear. I will sing a powerful song for you and your sisters and you must dance."

The young woman looked at the knothole in the tree, but Big Duck turned his head so that only his black hair could be seen and they believed his words. Then Big Duck began to pound on the inside of the tree with one hand, making a sound like a drum as he sang.

Wey hey hey ya
Wey hey hey ya
Wey hey hey ya
Wey ya ney!

So he sang and the young women danced. However, hearing the sound of the drumming, an older woman came down to the stream and saw them dancing.

"What are you doing?" the older woman said.

"There is a magical bear in that tree," the young women answered. "It is singing for us and we have to dance."

"Hunh!" said the older woman. "I wish to see that bear."

"No one must see the magical bear!" Big Duck shouted in a gruff voice, but the woman paid no attention. She went back to the village and returned with several men. They began to chop at the tree, even though they could hear the magical bear telling them to stop. Finally, with a loud crack, the tree split open. There stood Big Duck. Everyone began to laugh at him for his foolishness—except for the older woman, who was Big Duck's wife.

"My husband," she said, "this is the result of your friend, Sojy, is it not?"

Big Duck was so embarrassed that he could only nod his head. He followed his wife back to their lodge without saying a word. The next day he went hunting with the other men. From then on Big Duck did his best to work like the others and take care of his family. They say he never found his way to Trickster's Lodge again.

Then the boy and the Rabbit went over the cliffs on their
magic snowshoes and came safely down to the ground
below.

The Boy and the Kiwakweskwa (Sokoki)

Deep in the woods lived a terrible woman. She was a Kiwakweskwa, a monster who looked something like a human being. She had great strength, and her favorite food was human flesh. With her lived a human boy. He thought that he was her little brother, but the Kiwakweskwa had stolen him from his family when he was very small. She was fattening him up until he was big enough to eat.

This boy was a very good hunter. So, the Kiwakweskwa always sent him out to hunt rabbits. He had to shoot many of them. Not only did his Older Sister feed him very well, she also was very hungry herself. It was strange how hungry she was. He also thought it strange that she always kept her back to him. She never let him see her face and she only spoke in a whisper. Each morning she wakened him in the same way.

"Little Brother," she whispered. "Wake up. Come

115

over and let me feel how fat you are."

The boy rose and walked over to the place where Older Sister sat in the corner with her face turned away from him. She reached back her hand to pinch his arm and see how fat he felt. The boy did not like the way it felt when she did that, so he no longer held out his own arm for her to pinch. Instead he held out a piece of wood which was shaped like a little boy's skinny arm. He kept that piece of wood hidden under the skins where he slept.

"Hunh!" Older Sister whispered. "So skinny and tough. You are not yet fat and tender. Today you must go out and shoot more rabbits. Shoot more rabbits and make yourself fat, Little Brother."

The boy had killed so many rabbits that it was hard to find them now. Each day he had to go further and further to find them. One day, as he was hunting, he saw a large rabbit. He was about to shoot it when it turned and looked at him in a strange way. He lowered his bow and the rabbit spoke to him.

"Little Brother," the rabbit said. "You have killed enough rabbits. If you kill more rabbits, there will be none of us left."

"I am sorry," Little Brother said, "but my Older Sister told me I have to hunt many rabbits. She is always so hungry."

"Little Brother," the rabbit said, "I have come to warn you. That woman is not your sister. You should not obey her. She is not even a real human being. Her food is human beings. Each day when

116

you leave the lodge, she goes out and hunts for people to eat. She is just fattening you up before she eats you, too."

"How can I know this is true?" said the boy.

"Tonight," the rabbit said, "pretend to fall asleep. Cover your head, but watch what she does. Then you will see what she really is. Do as I say and you will realize she is a monster. Your own people are still alive and I can help you along the way to find them. I will make everything ready. Tomorrow you must meet me here in the forest. I will help you to escape."

When the boy went back to the lodge he told Older Sister that he could find no rabbits.

"Hunh!" she whispered. Her voice sounded fierce. "You must come over here and let me feel how fat you are."

As always, the boy held out the skinny stick which was shaped like the arm of a small boy and she pinched it with her fingers. The boy noticed how long and sharp her fingernails were.

"Hunh!" she whispered, "so skinny and tough. Perhaps you will never get fat and now you have brought no rabbits to eat."

"Older Sister," the boy said, "tomorrow I should be able to catch many rabbits. I will just go further into the forest where I haven't hunted before. Now I must go to sleep so I will be well rested for tomorrow."

The boy went over to the place where he slept and covered himself with a deerskin. But he had with him a small bone awl. He used it to make a hole in the skin just big enough so he could peek through it. Then he pretended to sleep, even though he kept watching his Older Sister.

Before long, Older Sister reached back with a stick and poked the fire so that some of the embers flew over towards the boy's sleeping place. "Hunh!" she whispered, "Little Brother, move quickly or you will be burned."

The boy, though, pretended to be asleep. His Older Sister reached into the corner and pulled out a huge pack which she kept covered with skins. She picked it up and shook it. "I am almost out of my food," she said. This time she did not whisper and the boy was frightened when he heard her voice. Her voice was as harsh as the howl of the North Wind. She reached into the pack and began to pull out her food. The boy was even more frightened when he saw what she was eating. He could hear the sound of her teeth crunching the bones as she ate with her back still turned to him. Finally she finished all of the food in her pack. She turned towards the boy to look at him where he slept.

"My boy is not going to get fatter," she said. "I will eat him tomorrow after he returns from hunting."

When she turned, the boy could see her face for the first time. That frightened him very much. His Older Sister had no lips and her teeth were as long and sharp as those of a wolf. She was not a person at all, she was a Kiwakweskwa, a monster of the forest who hunts human beings to eat.

Next morning, the boy rose very early. "Older Sister," he said, "I am going to hunt very deep in the forest. I am taking with me two pairs of mahkessen because I must be gone for four days. Not only will I bring back rabbits, I will also bring back a fat bear."

This pleased his sister. "Go, Little Brother," she whispered. "When you come back you will eat well and get very fat."

As soon as the boy went into the woods he began to run. He came to the place where his friend, the rabbit, was waiting.

"We must go very fast," the rabbit said. "You have done well, but the Kiwakweskwa will not wait four days. She will get hungry at the end of this day and start to follow." They ran all through that day and through the night. At dawn they came to some steep cliffs.

"Put on these snowshoes," said the rabbit, "we must go over these cliffs. The one who called herself your sister is close behind us."

The boy looked back and could see no one. Suddenly a great howl came from the north. It was the most terrible cry the boy had ever heard. In the midst of it he could hear the voice of the Kiwakweskwa.

"Little Brother,
Bad Little Brother
soon I will catch you
and eat you up."

That terrible voice frightened the boy so much that he could hardly move. His friend, the rabbit, came up to him and spoke.

"Hurry," the rabbit said. "Follow me."

Then the two of them went over the cliffs on their magic snowshoes and came safely down to the ground below. The Kiwakweskwa came to the top of the cliffs and tried to follow them, but she slipped and fell and was buried in falling rock.

The boy was happy, but his friend, the rabbit, spoke again.

"We must not stop," said the rabbit. "The one who called herself your sister is not truly dead. The Kiwakweskwa can come back to life three times before she is truly dead."

They ran and ran through that day and through the night. When morning came, they reached the bank of a wide rushing river.

"I must leave you here," the rabbit said. "Your friend, Heron, will help you across."

Just then they heard the howl of the Kiwakweskwa again. She had come back to life and dug her way out of the rocks.

"Little Brother,
Bad Little Brother,
soon I will catch you
and eat you up!"

The rabbit nudged the boy. "Go down to the river," he said. "Your friend, Heron, is waiting."

The boy ran down to the river. There by the edge stood a huge Heron.

"Grandfather," the boy said, "I need help to get across. An evil monster wants to eat me."

Heron began to sing:

> Very lovely legs has Heron,
> very lovely legs has Heron,
> very lovely legs has Heron,
> Heron's legs are pretty.

"Yes, Grandfather," the boy said, "your legs are very lovely and your neck is long and graceful, too."

The Heron nodded and stretched his leg across the river to make a bridge. "Grandson," Heron said, "your path is straight. Go across and continue on your way. When you come to your Grandfather Porcupine, he will show you where to go."

The boy crossed over on Heron's leg. When he reached the other side he began to run again. Heron pulled his leg back and waited.

When the Kiwakweskwa reached the bank she saw Heron standing there.

"Hurry up, Ugly Bird," she said. "Help me across so I can catch my Bad Little Brother."

Heron began to sing:

> Very lovely legs has Heron,
> very lovely legs has Heron,
> very lovely legs has Heron,
> Heron's legs are pretty.

"Legs all covered with mud," the Kiwakweskwa snarled. "And your neck is skinny, too. Hurry up and get me across or I'll break your ugly legs."

Heron put his leg across the river to make a bridge. The Kiwakweskwa started across. As soon as she reached the middle, Heron twisted his leg and she fell into the rushing water. It carried her downstream and over a big waterfall where she was killed on the rocks below.

Meanwhile, the boy kept running. He ran until his mahkessen were worn through and he had to put on his second pair. He ran through the day and through the night. Just at dawn, he came to the base of a mountain and in that mountain was a cave. In mouth of the cave, blocking its entrance, was a giant porcupine.

"Grandfather," the boy said, "show me the way to go. An evil monster is after me."

Porcupine began to sing:

> In a beautiful ledge is Porcupine's home,
> in a beautiful ledge is Porcupine's home,
> in a beautiful ledge is Porcupine's home,
> Porcupine's home is lovely.

"Yes, Grandfather," the boy said. "Your home is in a beautiful ledge. And your quills are as bright as the rays of the sun."

Porcupine moved aside so that the boy could enter his cave. "Come in and do not be afraid, Grandson," he said. "I will stop the Kiwakweskwa when she comes for you."

At the bottom of the rapids, the Kiwakweskwa came back to life.

"Wanh!" she said, spitting out water. "I have been asleep. Now I have to catch my Bad Little Brother." With a great howl, she took up the chase and before long she reached the cave where Porcupine sat blocking the mouth.

"Move aside, grubby quills," she said. "My Bad Little Brother is in your cave and I am hungry."

Porcupine began to sing:

"In a beautiful ledge is Porcupine's home,
in a beautiful ledge is Porcupine's home,
in a beautiful ledge is Porcupine's home,
Porcupine's home is lovely."

"Hanh!" the Kiwakweskwa snarled. "All covered with dirt is Porcupine's home and his quills are all grubby and dull. Now step aside."

Porcupine stepped aside and the Kiwakweskwa started into his cave. Just then, Porcupine shook his quills and swung his tail, piercing the Kiwakweskwa with his needles. Then he pushed her dead body out of his cave.

"Go quickly, Grandson," Porcupine said. "Follow this path from my cave. At the end of it you will find your real Grandfather."

The boy leaped out of the cave and found the path. He began to run. He ran all that day and through the night. When the dawn came, he found himself in front of a small lodge. An old man sat in front of the lodge with a small dog.

"Grandfather," the boy said, "I have come home."

The old man looked at the boy and did not recognize him. The Grandfather began to sing:

"Bad Dog, Bad Dog,
I give you this one.
Bad Dog, Bad Dog,
eat this one up."

Immediately, the small dog stood up. It shook itself and growled and it began to grow. It grew bigger and bigger until it was larger than a wolf. It grew bigger and bigger until it was larger than a bear. It ran towards the boy as if to eat him, but as soon as Bad Dog caught the boy's scent, he stopped. He began to whimper and he licked the boy's foot. He grew littler and littler until he was a small dog again. Then he rolled over on his back with his feet up in the air like a puppy.

The old man came close to the boy.

"Who are you?"

"I am your true grandson," the boy said. "I am running away from an evil woman who wants to eat me."

"Grandson!" the old man said, his voice filled with joy. "You have come back. The Kiwakweskwa stole you from me when you were very little. I did not know that you were still alive. Bad Dog is your dog and your parents are living. I shall take you to them."

Just then, a terrible howl filled the air. It was the Kiwakweskwa. The boy turned to look and saw the Kiwakweskwa enter the clearing where the Grandfather's lodge stood.

"Stand back, Grandson," the old man said. "She will not get you."

The old man rushed forward and began to fight with the Kiwakweskwa. They fought for a long time, but the evil monster was stronger and she began to win. The boy saw what he had to do. He began

124

to sing:

> "Bad Dog, Bad Dog,
> I give you this one.
> Bad Dog, Bad Dog,
> eat this one up."

Bad Dog stood up. He shook himself and he growled. He began to grow. Larger and larger he grew. He grew larger than a wolf, larger than a bear, and he kept growing until he was twice as big as the Kiwakweskwa. Then he leaped for the monster, and knocked her down. He tore her into small pieces and ate her up and she did not come back to life again.

The boy and his grandfather and Bad Dog went on to the village where the boy's parents were still living. All of them lived there happily together for a long time and when I left they were living there still.

There once was a young woman who liked nothing better than sitting and looking at the great mountain, Ktaadn. She thought, "If there was any man who was as strong and tall as Ktaadn, I would marry him."

The Son of Ktaadn
(Penobscot)

There once was a young woman who liked nothing better than sitting and looking at the great mountain, Ktaadn. Whether winter, when the mountain wore its robes of white, or spring when the lower slopes were bright green, she would sit and stare at Ktaadn. Many of the young men in her village wanted to marry her, but she was not interested in them. She would go out and pick blueberries on the slope of the mountain or sit on a hill where she could see the peak rising high above the land.

Her parents asked her what was wrong. "Why won't you marry one of the men in our village?" they said.

"If there were any man who was as strong and tall as Ktaadn," she said, "I would marry him." But there was no man like that in the village.

She made up a song about her loneliness and began to sit on that hill, singing the song softly to herself. One day, as she sat there singing her song, the

127

sun shone down on her so warmly that she fell asleep. When she woke, a man was standing before her. He was taller than any man she had ever seen and so handsome she thought she was dreaming. His eyebrows were as grey as stone and his cheeks looked like flint. He wore a robe of white skins about his shoulders.

"I am the one you called," he said. Then she knew that he was the spirit of the mountain itself. He held out his hand. "Will you come with me?"

The young woman took his hand and Ktaadn lifted her to her feet. The next thing she knew, she was standing with him high on the mountain itself. In front of them was the face of the cliff and they stood on a ledge of rock. Without a word, Ktaadn reached out and pressed his hand against the cliff. It opened like a door and the two of them went inside.

For four years, the young woman lived happily with her husband. She had everything she wanted there inside the great mountain. Her husband, Ktaadn, brought her fresh game to eat and she could pick berries on the mountain's slopes in the summer. Together she and her husband would walk on the mountaintop, looking out at the beautiful country all around. In the winter, her husband wrapped her in white robes to keep warm and their life together was good. After their first year together, she gave birth to a son and a daughter. They were strong, happy children and they looked just like other children except for one thing. Both of them had eyebrows as grey as stone.

At the end of that four years, the woman grew homesick.

"My husband," she said, "I want to visit my people. I want my children to know their grandparents."

"That is as it should be," Ktaadn said. "But when you return to your people, you must remember certain things. You can tell no one where you have been or who is the father of our children. Our children have great power. Whatever our daughter wishes will become true if she passes her hand across her mouth after making her wish. Whatever our son points his finger at will fall down dead if he wishes it. Remember, too, that you can return to me if your people do not treat you and our children well."

When the young woman returned to her village, her parents were pleased to see her. Everyone thought she had been carried away by enemies or killed by animals as she wandered on the mountain. However, her parents were not so pleased to see her two children. They grew very unhappy when she would not tell them who the father was.

"Are you ashamed of your husband?" her mother said.

"Is your husband an outcast from his people?" asked her mother.

But the young woman would not say.

It happened that there was a scarcity of food for the people that year. The berry bushes had not produced fruit. The streams were empty of fish. The woods were empty of game.

The young wife of Ktaadn saw this and felt very sad. She felt sadder still when some of the people in the village complained about her returning with extra mouths to feed when the people were about to starve.

"My children," she said, "do not feel badly about the way our people treat us. They would treat us better if there were plenty of food."

The little daughter thought about what her mother said. "I wish the bushes were covered with ripe berries," she said. Then she passed her hand over her mouth and the berry bushes became loaded down with ripe fruit.

The people of the village saw this and began to pick the berries. Everyone was much happier now, but still they did not treat the wife of Ktaadn and her two children any better.

"My children," the young wife said, "our people would treat us better if only there were fish to catch."

The little daughter thought about this. "I wish the streams were full of fat fish," she said. She passed her hand over her mouth and the streams became filled with fish.

The people saw this and began to catch the fish. They had a great feast, but they did not offer to share their food with the young wife of Ktaadn and the two children. Only her parents would give them food and the young wife grew very unhappy.

"My children," she said, "our people would be kinder if they had game to hunt."

"I wish there were many game animals in the woods all around us," the little daughter said. She passed her hand over her mouth and there were game animals all around.

The people saw this and began to hunt. They brought many animals back to the village. They had meat and skins and they were very happy, but still they ignored the young wife of Ktaadn and her two children.

"My children," she said, "I do not know what can make our people kinder to us."

Meanwhile, the little son of Ktaadn was playing as boys will play. As he played, he saw a deer pass by in the woods. He raised up his hand, and pointed his finger at the deer.

"Let that deer fall dead," he said. And the deer fell down. He dragged the deer back to the lodge of his grandparents and the whole family had food to eat, even though no one but his mother knew how the small boy had gotten the deer.

The next day, the boy was out playing again. This time he saw a moose. Again he pointed his finger and again he spoke. "Let that moose fall dead." As soon as he spoke, the moose fell down. Then the boy dragged the moose back to the lodge. His grandparents were very surprised, but the young wife of Ktaadn still did not explain how her boy had gotten the moose.

It went on this way for a time. The boy provided

plenty of food for his family. However, the people of the village still did not treat them well. The other children made fun of the boy and his sister for their strange eyebrows and their lack of a father.

One day, when the boy and his sister were playing, a group of children from the village began to taunt them. Then one of the village boys threw a stone and struck the boy on his forehead.

The son of Ktaadn pointed his finger at the boy who threw the stone. But before he could say anything, his sister spoke.

"I wish we were back with my father," she said. She passed her hand over her mouth and the two of them disappeared.

As soon as she heard what had happened, the young wife of Ktaadn went back up the mountain to find her children and her husband. Not long after they left, the berries began to dry up, the fish left the streams and the game went away. The people of the village suffered a great deal, but no one could help them. The wife of Ktaadn and her two children never returned.

On stormy nights, the sound of thunder rolls from the great peak. Some say that it is the two children, happy to be back with their father and playing inside the mountain.

When he tried to follow her she turned into a deer and disappeared into the cedars.

The Deer Wife
(Penobscot)

There once was a man called Zazigoda or The Lazy One. Whenever he went hunting with the other men he would find a place and go to sleep while the other men looked for game.

One day, while they were hunting deep in the woods the other men said, "Where is Zazigoda?" They went and looked and found him asleep under a cedar tree. They were tired now of his being so lazy. They went away and left him there.

When Zazigoda awoke it was very dark. He was hungry, but he had no food. He was not sure how to find his way out of the woods because he had always been careless about tracking, only following the other hunters. "Here is where I shall starve," he said. "This is because I have not helped others."

Then suddenly, a woman stood before him. She was dressed in brown deerskin and her hair was long and brown. "Come with me," she said and Zazigoda followed her to her lodge deep in the woods. She gave him food and took care of him.

The next day she told him how to hunt for moose. "Wait by the lake. Sing this song," she said. "Then blow through this birchbark horn. The moose will come to you and you can shoot it with your arrows." He went out and did as she told him and that night they feasted on the meat of the moose and she made him a robe of the moose skin.

The following day she told him how to hunt for bear. "Go to the berry bushes. Sing this song and wait by the trail. The bear will come to you and you can shoot it with your arrows." Again Zazigoda did as she said. That night they ate bear meat and the woman made for him a robe from the bear skin. So it went for a long time. Zazigoda grew fat and the lodge was filled with skins.

The woman told him how to hunt for every animal in the forest except one. "You must not hunt for the deer, my husband," she told him and Zazigoda agreed.

At last Zazigoda became lonely for his people. "I must go and visit them," he said.

"Go ahead," said the woman, "but I shall remain here. Take the skins and the meat with you and share it with the people. Say nothing about me. Stay until it is the time again for hunting and then come back to me."

Zazigoda did as she said. His relatives rejoiced when they saw him coming with the meat and all the skins. He was a different looking man now. The unmarried women all wanted to dance with him, but Zazigoda paid no attention to them. He stayed, sharing all that he had with the people and then, when the season to hunt came again, he went alone into the woods to the lodge of the woman. He hunted throughout the winter and when spring came the woman gave birth to a daughter. Once more she told him to take the food and furs to his relatives and once again she stayed in the woods, this time with their child.

Again his relatives were happy to see him and again many of the unmarried women wanted to marry him. All of his relatives told him that a fine man such as he should marry. He refused them three times, but finally on the fourth time he consented. He married one of the women in the village and for a time they lived together happily. But when the season to hunt came he went again into the woods.

When he came to the lodge of his forest wife, he found it was empty. He called and there was no answer. Then he saw her standing at the edge of the forest. "You have forgotten me," she said. "No longer can I live with you. You will still be able to hunt as you did before, but never must you kill a deer." Then she was gone.

The man was sad to see her go and not to see their baby daughter, but he did as she said. He hunted and stayed alone in the lodge and killed many animals but never killed a deer. He went back with the meat and skins to his wife in the village. She was not pleased.

"Why have you brought me no deer meat?" she

said. "That is all that I want."

He tried to refuse, but she continued to ask and beg him. Even his relatives told him that he should do as his wife asked. At last he went and did as she said. He went into the woods to hunt deer. He saw a doe and a fawn and shot the fawn with his arrow. Suddenly his forest wife was there standing before him.

"You have done what I asked you never to do," she said. "Now you have killed our daughter."

Zazigoda looked down and saw that it was so. He turned to the woman but she was running away from him. When he tried to follow her she turned into a deer and disappeared into the cedars.

Slender Reed climbed onto Jodikwado's flat head and grasped his horn. Then, turning his head towards the mainland, he began to swim.

Jodíkwado and the Young Wife (Mahican)

Long ago, there was a young woman named Slender Reed who married a man from another village. In her own village, it was the custom that the husband would come and live in the lodge of the wife's mother. However, her new husband's people followed a different way. So, because she loved her new husband very much, the young wife went to his village, which was in the land of the Mohegan people close to the big river.

Things went well for a time, but the man's sister grew very jealous of the attention Slender Reed received from everyone. Finally, the sister-in-law's mind grew so twisted that she decided to rid herself of her rival. It was the season when the berries were ripe and she took her berry basket and went to Slender Reed.

"Sister," she said, "come with me to gather berries."

Slender Reed quickly agreed. This was the first show of friendliness she had received from her sister-in-law. The two women went down to the big river.

"We shall go out to Manansis, the little island," said the sister-in-law. "The berries are better out there." Then she pulled her canoe down to the water, and she and Slender Reed climbed in.

When they reached the island, the sister-in-law handed the berry basket to Slender Reed. "Here," she said, "you go ahead. I am going to rest here by the water for a while. The best berries are on the other side of the island. If you are hungry, eat some of those berries. You can eat as many as you want and there will still be more than enough left."

Slender Reed began to walk to the other side of the island. It was important to please the sister of her husband. As soon as she was out of sight, the jealous sister-in-law took the canoe and paddled back to the mainland. When she reached the shore, she scratched her hands with briers and tore her clothes. Then she ran back to the village and fell down on the ground near her brother's lodge, calling for help.

Her brother came running out. "What is wrong? Where is my wife?"

"Ahh-ahh," said the jealous sister, "a terrible thing has happened. We were picking blueberries in the fields away from the river when four enemy warriors came out of the forest. I told Slender Reed to run, but she just stood there and was taken captive. I am afraid you will never see your wife again."

Meanwhile, Slender Reed had reached the other side of the island. But she quickly saw that all of the berries there were white. Her mother had taught her that white berries are always poisonous and so she did not pick any of them or eat them. So, she kept walking around the island until she came back to the place where her sister-in-law had left her. There on the sand were the marks of the canoe, but the canoe was nowhere to be seen. She was stranded on the island. The current of the river was strong and the distance to the shore was too great for her to swim. There was nothing for her to eat and she knew that her sister-in-law had left her there to die. She sat down on the sand and wept.

Before long, the sun began to set. Darkness crept over the island and Slender Reed became afraid. Some said that Manansis, the little island, was an enchanted place. People sometimes looked out at night across the river and saw dancing lights, even though no one lived on the little island. Slender Reed looked for a place to hide herself. There, close to the beach, was an old hollow log. She crept inside it and finally went to sleep.

It was late in the night when she was wakened by a strange whooping cry. It came from somewhere out in the river. There was a hole in the log near her face and she peered through it, looking out towards the water. Strange lights were flickering and dancing over the waves. As she watched, they came closer and closer until finally they formed a circle on the beach close to her hiding place. The lights grew brighter and brighter and then they changed into shapes which were neither human beings nor animals. Then they began to speak.

"Brothers," one of them said, "we have come together in council to decide how to help this woman. Her sister-in-law has tricked her and left her on our island. If she eats the berries she will die, but if she does not eat she will starve. What can we do?"

"We must carry her back to the land," another one said, its voice as deep as the beat of a drum.

"I shall carry her!" said yet another one.

"Nda, Brother," said the first speaker, "you are not strong enough."

"Then I shall do it," said the one with the deep voice.

"Nda," said the first speaker, "you are too frightening to look at. She would run and hide from you."

So they spoke for some time until finally the tallest of the beings rose up and spoke. His voice was soft, yet very clear. "I have the power to carry her," he said. "Even if the Thunders come, I will carry her to the shore."

"So it will be," said the first speaker.

Then the shapes began to fade away and in their places the lights flickered once more. They danced up from the sand and began to move over the water. As she watched the lights disappear, Slender

142

Reed found herself growing more and more weary. Her eyes closed and she slept.

The next morning, just at sunrise, she heard a voice calling her from the edge of the water. She crawled out of the log and went down to the beach. There, with its head and half of its body out of the water, was a huge serpent. It was bigger than a great tree and from its head grew a single horn. Its scales shone like white and purple wampum. Slender Reed looked into its eyes and, despite its great size, she was not afraid, for its gaze was gentle and mild.

"Little Sister," the great snake said, "I am Jodikwado. I have come to help you. Will you trust me?"

"I will trust you," Slender Reed said. "Tell me what to do."

"First you must break four branches from the willows. You must use them as switches to encourage me when I do not swim fast enough. Then you must climb onto my head and hold onto my horn. Do not lose faith and you shall reach the shore."

Slender Reed did as Jodikwado said. She broke branches from the willows and made four switches. She climbed onto his flat head and grasped his horn. Then, turning his head towards the mainland, Jodikwado began to swim. His body moved smoothly through the water without making a ripple. However, as soon as they set out, a wind began to blow across the water.

"Little Sister," Jodikwado said, "are clouds forming in the sky?"

Slender Reed looked up. "Yes," she said. "There are black clouds to the west."

"Use the first switch," said Jodikwado, "Strike me hard so that I will swim faster."

Slender Reed did as he said. She began to use the first willow switch, striking it back against the great snake's sides and he swam faster through the waves. Now the little island was far behind them, but the wind was blowing stronger.

"Little Sister," Jodikwado said, "are the clouds coming closer?"

Slender Reed looked up. "Yes," she said, "the black clouds are moving very fast. They are almost overhead."

"Use the second switch," Jodikwado said. "I am afraid that the Thunder Beings have seen me. They are my enemies and will try to kill me."

Slender Reed took the second switch and struck it against Jodikwado's side. He swam even faster still and now they were almost half way to the shore. However, the black clouds were overhead and Slender Reed heard the first rumbles of thunder.

"Quickly," Jodikwado said, "use the third switch, Little Sister."

As Slender Reed began to use the third switch, the rain began to strike them and the wind blew so hard that she could barely hold onto Jodikwado's horn with her one arm. But she continued to switch his sides and they moved faster still. Now the shore was close. Suddenly, a great bolt of lightning came out of the sky. The Thunder Being had fired one of his arrows. But the arrow did not strike the great snake. Instead, it struck a floating log and split it in half.

"Use the fourth switch," Jodikwado shouted, "quickly or we shall both be killed."

Slender Reed took the last switch and began to strike it back against Jodikwado's side. But he was no longer moving as swiftly. In fact, he was hardly moving at all in the water, even though the shore was close by.

"I must dive now," Jodikwado shouted, "Leap off, Little Sister!" Just then another bolt of lightning struck the water close by and the great snake dove. Slender Reed let go of his horn and jumped off, certain that she was about to drown. However, as soon as she put her feet down, they touched the bottom and she was able to wade to the mainland. Overhead, the sky was already clearing and the sun began to shine. She looked back towards the water and saw no sign of Jodikwado, but she felt something in her hand. She looked down and saw it was the very tip of Jodikwado's horn. It was a great gift, for it was known to everyone that the horn of the underwater serpent was very powerful and could be used to cure the sick.

"Brother," Slender Reed called out towards the river, "thank you for saving me. I shall burn tobacco for you on the bank of this river each year at this time."

Then Slender Reed began to walk back to the village of her husband. She was not sure what she would find, but she had already vowed to herself that she would say nothing of the evil her sister-in-law had done. When she reached the village, she saw many people gathered around the lodge of her husband. No one recognized her, for her face was streaked with mud and her clothing was torn and wet.

"What is wrong?" she said.

"Ah," an old woman said, "the man in this lodge is sick at heart because his wife was stolen by our enemies. It seems that he is about to die."

Slender Reed pushed through the crowd. There, on a bearskin, lay her husband. She came close to him and touched his chest with the piece of Jodikwado's horn. As soon as she did so her husband sat up.

"My wife," he said, with joy in his voice, "is it truly you?"

From the back of the crowd, the jealous sister-in-law watched the reunion. She listened to Slender Reed tell her story. She told how she had been left on the island, but she made no mention of her sister-in-law. She told how the great snake had come to help her and given her the magical horn after saving her life.

"Kwe-yoh!" the sister-in-law said, "it is not fair. I am the one who should have such a gift." Then the sister-in-law went down to the river and climbed into her canoe. She paddled out to the island, stepped ashore, and then pushed her boat out into the river.

"Oh!" she cried loudly, "I have lost my boat. Surely I will die here." She sat down on the shore and pretended to weep. Then, when it became dark, she crept into the hollow log and waited. Before long, the dancing lights came across the water and settled on the shore.

"Someone is asking for help," said the first speaker.

"I know who she is," said the one with the deep voice.

"Let me give her what she deserves," said a third voice.

"No, brother," said the first speaker, "you are too weak."

"I shall take care of her in the morning," said a soft clear voice.

"That is good," said the first speaker.

Then the lights darted away over the water and were gone.

"Hunh," the sister-in-law said to herself. "That does not sound like what Slender Reed told the people they said. But, still, tomorrow they will bring me my gift."

When the morning came, the sister-in-law was standing by the water.

"Come along," she called. "Where is the one who is going to help me?"

Then the great snake lifted his head out of the water. It frightened her when he appeared so suddenly, but she remembered what had happened with Slender Reed.

"I am Jodikwado," the great snake said. "Are you truly in need of help?"

"Of course I am," said the sister-in-law, who was collecting a great armload of switches from the willows. "Now put your head down here so I can get on."

Jodikwado did as she said and soon he was swimming through the water. On his back, the sister-in-law was switching him as hard as she could, but he did not go faster. Before long she had used up all the switches, but the mainland was still far away. Then she pulled out her knife and began trying to cut a piece off of Jodikwado's horn. She hacked away at it, but only succeeded in breaking the blade.

"Are there clouds overhead?" Jodikwado said.

The sister-in-law looked up. The sky was clear. "If it will make you swim any faster, yes. Yes, there are many clouds. Now hurry and get me to shore."

"Are the clouds closer?" said Jodikwado.

The sister-in-law looked up. The sky was still clear. "Yes," she said. "They are very close. Now take me to shore and give me what I deserve."

"Do you hear thunder?" said Jodikwado.

"Yes," said the sister-in-law, "the thunder is very loud."

"Then I must dive," said Jodikwado, and with that he dove deep into the water, leaving the sister out in the middle of the river.

No one in her village ever found out what happened to the jealous sister-in-law, but few people missed her. And Slender Reed and her husband lived there together happily all of their lives. So the story goes.

The Ktchiawaasak leaned against the trees to rest. The trees broke and the great beasts fell over on their sides and could not get up again. Snowy Owl shot each of them in the bottoms of their feet and killed them.

Snowy Owl and the Great White Hare (Abenaki)

Long ago, in a quiet village far to the north, there lived a man and a woman who had one son. They named this boy Snowy Owl, because there were many of those birds where they lived. Also, they wanted that bird to be the boy's guardian.

One winter, the man decided to take his family across the divide into the mountains where the hunting would be better. For a time, things went well there. Then the father and mother became sick. Each day they grew sicker and nothing that Snowy Owl did could help them. One night, the father called Snowy Owl to him.

"My son," he said, "your mother and I will soon walk the spirit road. You must send your animal helper, the white owl, to your grandmother. Then she will come for you and take care of you."

Snowy Owl did as his father said. That night, a white owl appeared to his grandmother as she

151

dreamed.

"You must go to your grandson in the mountains," the white owl said.

When she woke, the grandmother put her pack on her back and began the long journey. She went to the place in the mountains where her husband had built a lodge many seasons ago. There she found her grandson waiting.

"Grandmother," he said, "my mother and father have walked the spirit road."

The grandmother stayed there with Snowy Owl and cared for him. He was a strong young man and learned things quickly. At last, the time came when she knew he was ready. She took out a birch bark basket and opened it.

"Grandson," she said, "this was your grandfather's bow."

She took out a bundle wrapped in a skin and drew from it the pieces of an ivory bow and fastened them together.

"Grandson," she said, "these are the heads for your arrows."

She took out another bundle wrapped in a skin. Within it were ivory arrowheads.

"Grandson," she said, "whatever you shoot at with these, you will hit. You must talk to the arrows as you shoot them and they will do as you say."

Snowy Owl took the magic ivory bow and the arrowheads. He took the old heads from his arrows and fastened on the ivory heads. Then he stepped outside.

"Arrow," he said, "hit that cone at the top of the tallest spruce." He shot the arrow and it struck the tiny cone and knocked it to the ground.

Snowy Owl was pleased and he looked around for another target to hit.

"Arrow," he said, drawing back his bow and aiming again, "hit the middle tail feather on that hawk flying high overhead." He let the arrow go. It flew high in the air and disappeared from sight. When it fell to the ground, the tail feather of a hawk was stuck to the tip of the arrow. Snowy Owl was very pleased.

"Now," his grandmother said, "you must go back to our village. I will stay here, for I am an old woman and may not have much longer to live. As you travel, Grandson, be careful. I am afraid that the witches who killed your parents may try to kill you also. We are close to the land of the Great White Hare and I believe he and his wife are the ones who caused them to die. His wife is a witch and has seven daughters. Any man who tries to marry one of them suffers an awful fate. On their marriage night, the daughters always offer to comb the hair of their husband. Their combs are magic and they comb out the man's brains and eat them. Then they send the man farther to the north where the Great White Hare waits in his barren land. The Great White Hare changes them into hares and they remain under his rule forever."

"I will be careful, Grandmother," Snowy Owl said, but in his heart he vowed that he would seek out the Great White Hare one day and avenge the death of his parents.

Then Snowy Owl began to travel to the south. When he came to his people's village, they were glad to see him. With his magic bow, he soon became the chief hunter. It was now the summer time and the people noticed that something strange was happening. The lakes, which were fed by the springs, were getting lower and lower. Scouts were sent to the springs to discover what was wrong, but none of them ever returned. The people were afraid that the lakes would dry up and they would have no water. They continued to send out scouts, but still none returned.

Snowy Owl decided to go and see for himself what was wrong. The next time that scouts were sent out, Snowy Owl went, too. He did not go with the others. He chose his way carefully and kept watch as he went. He did not follow the trails the other scouts took. When he came to a mountain, he climbed to its top and looked out. He could see a long way over the countryside. The land was flat except for many small grassy hills close by the trails to the springs. From his place on the mountaintop, Snowy Owl could see the other scouts on those trails.

When the scouts reached the grassy hills, the hills began to move! They were not hills at all, but huge animals with long teeth. The scouts shot their arrows at the huge animals, but the animals were too big and there were too many of them. All of the scouts were trampled by the great beasts.

Snowy Owl had heard of these creatures from his parents. They were the Ktchiawaasak, the giant animals. Even with his magic bow and arrows, he was not certain that he could kill them. The only place where an arrow could pierce them was on the bottom of their feet. He continued to watch from the mountaintop. He saw that the huge beasts had very stiff legs. At night they did not lie down. Instead, they rested against big trees. The bark was worn off those trees where the great beasts leaned.

Snowy Owl watched from that mountain and from other mountains around the plain throughout the next day and saw what the Ktchiawaasak did. They grazed the grass and bushes and ate the bark off the smaller trees. Wherever they fed, they ate everything and the earth became dry. They drank much water from the springs and wallowed in the mud. It was clear that they were the reason the lakes were drying up. Somehow, Snowy Owl would have to kill them.

He decided to go back to his village and tell the people. No more scouts should be sent to the springs. The Ktchiawaasak would kill them, too. Then he could make a plan to destroy the monsters. He began to travel back towards his village. As he traveled, he made a great circle to avoid the Ktchiawaasak. As he did so, he entered the land of the Great White Hare.

It was late in the day when Snowy Owl came to

a camp where an old woman lived with her seven daughters.

"Son-in-law," the old woman said, "welcome to our lodge. You can spend the night with us. My daughters have no husbands. Choose one of them to marry."

Snowy Owl looked at the seven daughters. To their surprise, he went to the youngest of the daughters. No man had ever chosen her before. He looked at her and something went out of her eyes.

"This is the one I choose," he said, taking her by the hand.

This youngest daughter was not like her mother and her older sisters. She did not want Snowy Owl to suffer the fate of all the other men who lost their brains.

"Listen," she whispered to him, "my mother and my sisters are witches. Trust me and I will help you." Then she began to sew seven caps.

"What are you making?" the old woman said.

"I am making new caps for you and my sisters. You can wear them tonight when I marry my new husband."

That amused the old woman. Throughout the day, the youngest daughter worked on the caps while the old woman and the older daughters waited for the night. During the day, they had no special power, but when night came, they could do many evil things. When the sun began to set, the youngest daughter finished the seven caps and handed them to her mother and her older sisters.

"Now," she said, "put on your new caps and I will marry my new husband."

As soon as they put the caps on, the old woman and her six daughters all fell asleep.

"We must run now," the youngest daughter said to Snowy Owl. Together the two of them ran through the night. The six older sisters and the old woman slept soundly as they ran. However, halfway through the night, the old woman rolled over and the cap fell off her head. She woke and leaped to her feet.

"You cannot escape me," she screamed and began to follow the trail left by Snowy Owl and her youngest daughter.

Far ahead, Snowy Owl and the youngest daughter heard that awful scream and ran harder. As they ran, they came to a big lodge and saw a kind-looking old man sitting in front of it.

"Kwe, Grandfather," White Owl said.

"Come into my lodge," said the old man. "I am Mesatawe and I will help you." Thus they knew that the old man was Great Star, the last star to remain in the sky at the end of the night, the lazy one who sleeps late in the morning.

Snowy Owl and the youngest daughter went and hid in the back of his lodge. Just as they did so, the old woman arrived.

"Old Man," she howled, "you must let me into your lodge."

"Yes," Mesatawe said, "I will do so. But first I have to dress myself." Then, very slowly, he began to put on his clothes. The night was almost over and the old woman was impatient.

"Hurry," she howled, "the sun will rise soon."

"I am hurrying," Mesatawe said, "I am just putting on my leggings."

Now the sky was red in the east where the sun was about to come up.

"Hurry," the old woman howled again, "when the sun rises I lose my power."

"Yes," Mesatawe said, "I am just putting on my shirt."

The birds were beginning their first songs and the glow of the coming sunrise was brighter now.

"Hurry!" the old woman howled, "there is not much time."

"I am hurrying," Mesatawe said, "I am just putting on my moccasins. There, now I am dressed." Mesatawe opened the door and stepped out. Just as he did so, the sun rose. The old woman lost her power and fell again into a deep sleep.

"Run further that way." Mesatawe said to Snowy Owl and the youngest daughter, "There the seven Thunder brothers will help you."

Snowy Owl and the youngest daughter ran all through the day. At last, they came to the caves in the north where the Thunders lived.

"Grandfathers," Snowy Owl called, "we were sent this way by Great Star. We need your help."

"Open your eyes a little and see who it is," said the oldest of the Thunder Brothers to the youngest Thunder Brother. He opened his eyes just a crack and the sound of thunder rumbled about them, but lightning did not strike.

"It is Snowy Owl and the youngest daughter," the Thunder Brother said.

"Let them in," said the oldest Thunder Brother. "We will help them."

Snowy Owl and the youngest daughter stayed in the cave of the seven Thunder Brothers throughout that day. When night came, once more they heard the howling cry of the old woman when she woke and began to follow their trail.

"You cannot escape me!" she screamed.

Before long, she reached the cave.

"Let me in," she howled.

"Who is it?" said the oldest of the Thunder Brothers.

"Can't you see, stupid one!" the old woman howled. "All of you open your eyes and you will see who I am!"

Then the seven Thunder Brothers opened their eyes. Lightning flashed forth and thunder rumbled all around them. When they closed their eyes again, Snowy Owl and the youngest daughter came out of the cave. The old woman was gone.

Without their mother to guide them in evil, the six older sisters no longer combed the brains from men. The Great White Hare lost his power and grew smaller and smaller until he became only another hare himself. The other hares which had been under his rule began to drift down from the northland and are found throughout the land to this day.

Snowy Owl and the youngest daughter started on their way back to his village. Their flight from the old woman had brought them close to the place where the great beasts lived. Snowy Owl told his new wife of the trouble the Ktchiawaasak were causing for his people.

"I know how we can kill them," the youngest sister said. She told Snowy Owl her plan and he saw that it was a good one.

The two of them waited until the Ktchiawaasak left their sleeping places. Then Snowy Owl and the youngest sister slipped in and began to cut through the trunks of the trees where the great beasts leaned as they slept. They cut each tree almost all of the way through.

That night, the Ktchiawaasak came back to their sleeping places. They leaned against the trees to rest. The trees broke and the great beasts fell over on their sides and could not get up again. Then, with his magic ivory bow, Snowy Owl shot each of them in the bottoms of their feet and killed them. He killed all of them. There are no longer any such beasts today, though sometimes people dig up their bones.

After that, Snowy Owl and the youngest daughter went to his village. The people welcomed them and made Snowy Owl their chief. And they were all living happily there when I left them.

Horned Owl was lonely. Aside from his old aunt, he was all alone in the world. So he decided to look for a wife.

The Owl Husband
(Penobscot)

Horned Owl was lonely. Aside from his old aunt, he was all alone in the world. So he decided to look for a wife. He traveled around for some time, trying to find someone. Then, one day as he sat in a tree outside a certain village, a young woman passed him on her way to the stream to get water. Horned Owl looked at her and knew she was the one he wanted to marry.

This young woman, though, was both beautiful and proud. Many young men wanted to marry her, but she did not want any of them. Her father asked her what kind of man she wanted to marry.

"I will marry the first man," she said, "who is able to make the fire in our lodge burn brighter by spitting on it."

Many young men tried to pass this test, but all of them failed. No matter how often they tried, whenever they would spit on the fire it would burn lower.

Horned Owl saw all this and went to his aunt. He

asked her for help. His aunt made up a special potion, using pine pitch.

"Put this in your mouth," she said. "Then spit it onto the fire."

Horned Owl went into the village and went to the lodge of the proud young woman. Many of the tribal elders were then sitting around the fire, which was just barely burning. Horned Owl went straight to the old man.

"Father-in-law," he said, "it is true that I can marry your daughter if I make the fire burn brighter by spitting into it?"

"That is so," the old man said. "I promise in front of the elders and our chief that the first man who makes the fire burn brighter by spitting into it shall marry my daughter."

Horned Owl went up to the fire and spit into it. The embers began to burn brighter. He spit again and they blazed up into flame. He spit a third time and the flames roared up to the top of the lodge.

"That is enough" the old man said. He took his daughter by the hand. "My daughter will marry you. You have passed her test."

The young woman, though, was not sure about this strange man. He was good-looking and tall, but something was different about him. He was wearing a tall head-dress and as she stood next to him, she reached out and pulled it from his head. As soon as she did so, his ears stuck up out of his hair.

"Look," she shouted. "This one is not a man. I said I would marry the first man who passed my test."

All of the men looked at him with fear and suspicion. Horned Owl walked out of the lodge, leaving his wife behind him. He changed himself back into an owl and flew off into the trees.

He did not go far away, though. He was still lonely. He stayed close to the village and watched his wife, trying to think of some way to win her back. Now she no longer said she would marry the first man who could spit into the fire and make it burn brighter. Instead, she said she would marry the man who was the best provider.

Horned Owl waited for a few days. Then he changed his appearance. He made himself look younger and more handsome. He dressed in fine clothing and he combed his thick hair over his ears so that they were hidden and would not stand up. He went hunting and killed two moose which he dragged into the village. As the people gathered around, he spoke.

"I come from a village not far from here. All of us are great hunters in my village. Now I am looking for a wife. I would like to make my lodge in your village and share my game with you all whenever I hunt."

The people were impressed. They helped him skin the moose and they planned a big feast that night. Horned Owl was feeling happy. He was sure he would be able to show his wife that he was the best provider and she would agree to marry him again. That night, even the proud girl and her family came to the feast. When she looked at this new man, though, she thought there was something strange about him. After everyone had eaten, she stood up.

"Let us all tell stories," she said. "I will be the first."

"That is a good idea," Horned Owl said. "I would like to hear a story." Everyone else agreed.

"My story," the proud young woman said, "has to be told in a whisper, everyone will have to uncover their ears and lean forward to listen."

Everyone except for Horned Owl did as she said. They brushed their hair back from their ears and leaned forward.

"I can hear very well," Horned Owl said, "I don't have to uncover my ears."

"Then I cannot tell my story," the proud young woman said.

"Uncover your ears, uncover your ears," everyone said.

"I am the one who provided this feast," Horned Owl said, but no one listened to him. They began to shout.

"Uncover your ears! Uncover your ears!"

Horned Owl stood up and threw back his hair. His ears stood up straight and everyone grew silent. His eyes glowed yellow in the firelight. Then, without saying a word, he walked out into the night and flew away.

Now Horned Owl was very sad. He felt that this young woman would never accept him. He watched her each evening from the trees near the village and his heart was heavy. She no longer came to the spring for water. She and her parents were afraid that the strange one who wanted to marry her might carry her off if she left the village. Horned Owl could only see her from a distance.

At last, he went into the forest and made himself a flute from the branch of a cedar tree. He sat there every evening near the spring where he first saw the proud young woman. He sat there and played his flute, pouring all of the loneliness and sorrow from his heart into every note.

One evening, the proud young woman could stand it no longer. She wanted to walk outside the village. Surely, she was in no danger now from that strange one who had tried to marry her. And even though his ears were not like those of a human being, he had been very tall and handsome. She was certain that he would never return again. She left her lodge and took the path to the spring.

As she walked, she thought she heard music. As she grew closer to the spring, the music grew louder. It was the sound of a flute and it was the most beautiful song she had ever heard. It was so filled with longing and loneliness, that it filled her own heart. She looked around, but could not see who was playing.

"Whoever is playing this song," she said, "I will take him gladly for my husband."

As soon as he heard those words, Horned Owl flew down from the tree. He carried the proud young woman off with him to his lodge. Although he was not like others, she learned to love him and the two of them lived happily together for a long time.

The young man plays in the water with his wife's sister.

The Water Woman
(Passamaquoddy)

There was a young man who used to like nothing better than to sit by the ocean and watch the waves. While the other young men did the things young men like to do, he would sit and imagine what it was like beneath the water.

Some of the girls tried to catch his interest, but he paid no attention to them. "His mind is lost in the old days," the girls said and they left him alone.

There was one place in particular where the young man liked to sit and watch the water. It was a sheltered cove where the beach was wide and level at the edge of the deep water. Many trees grew there and the stones of the tall cliffs glittered with many colors. One day, as he sat in that place, the young man grew tired. He lay down beside a log and soon fell asleep.

He did not know how long he slept, but he was wakened by the sound of voices. They were the voices of young women, but the voices sounded lovelier than those of any of the girls in the town.

"Throw me the ball, sisters! Throw it to me," called a voice which was as sweet as the song of the hermit thrush.

The young man sat up very slowly and looked over the top of the log. The tide had gone out and there on the wide beach were people. They were four young women, all dressed in old time clothing which glistened as brightly as the stones of the cliffs. They were playing with a blue ball.

All of the young women were graceful in their movements, but one of them—who appeared to be the youngest—was so beautiful that the young man knew he wanted to speak to her. He stood up from behind the log. As soon as he did so, the four young women saw him. They dropped their ball, ran to the water, and leaped in. He ran after them, but they vanished beneath the surface and they did not come up again. He turned to look at the ball they had dropped, but where there had been a ball there was now just a small pool of water.

Unlike most of the other young men today, he still liked to listen to the old people telling stories. So it was that he knew right away what had happened. The four young women were water people and lived in the ocean. If you could catch hold of one of the water people when they were on the land, they would have to grant whatever you wished.

Now that he knew this was the place where those four sisters came to play, he decided to wait and try to catch them. He did not have enough power to follow them under the water, but there were other things he could do. He went home and made medi-cine. Then he came back to the beach and made himself small enough to hide under the folded leaf of the Jack-in-the-pulpit.

He waited there as the tide began to go out. When he heard the voices of the four young women, he lifted the leaf of the flower and looked out. They were playing ball again, but the flower was not close enough to shore for him to jump out and catch one of them. He especially wanted to catch the youn-gest sister. Just then the ball rolled across the beach towards the flower. As the youngest sister ran to get it, he started to climb out of the flower. The youngest sister, though, was very sharp-eyed. She saw him and shouted to her sisters. All four of them ran and jumped into the waves and were gone.

The young man went back home and thought about what he could do. This time, when he came back to the beach, he made himself even smaller and hid inside the hollow of a reed growing right next to the shore. Now he would be close enough to catch the youngest one and make her grant his wish.

He waited patiently. When the tide went out he heard their voices again. "No one is here, sisters. Let us play."

The sound of their ball-playing came closer and closer. At last, he thought they were close enough and he leaped out of the reed. The four sisters saw him and ran. The youngest sister was closest to the ocean and leaped in before he could catch her, but he was just able to grasp the arm of one of the others before she could reach the water.

"Now," he said, "you must grant my wish."

"That is so," the water woman answered.

"My wish is to marry a woman who lives beneath the waves," he said.

"I am already married," the water woman replied. "But if you let me go, I will bring my youngest sister to you tomorrow and she will be your wife."

"That is my wish," the young man said.

When the next day came, the water woman kept her promise. She returned with her youngest sister. The girl smiled at the young man and they went together back to his home.

They lived together happily for some time. A year passed and the young wife gave birth to a son.

"Husband," she said, "I wish to go back and visit my parents. They have never seen their grandson."

"You may go," he said, "if you will take me with you."

So the two of them went down to the water with their child. The woman began to wade into the water, but the husband held back.

"Do not worry," she said. "Follow me and we will go to the land of my people."

The man did as his wife said. He waded into the water behind her and soon he was under the waves. There, in front of them, was a trail. He looked around and he could see that the place around them was much like the world above the waves. They walked a long way until they looked down on a beautiful village in a valley below. There were many trees lifting taller than any trees he had ever seen before.

"This is where my parents live," the wife said. "My father is the chief of this land."

Now the people in the village began to come out. The young man recognized his wife's three sisters, but they looked different than they had looked on land. Instead of legs, they now had the tails of fish. All of the people in the village were that way. He looked over at his wife, but she had not changed. She saw him looking and she smiled.

"Now that I have married a man of the upper world, I can no longer be like the rest of my people, even when I come to visit them."

A dignified old man approached them, his wife by his side.

"These are my parents," the wife said. Then the old chief and his wife embraced their daughter and her husband and their baby son.

The three of them stayed for almost a year among the water people. The young man learned that his father-in-law had power over all of the fish in the sea and he saw many wonderful things. One day, though, he knew that he could stay no longer. Now he was homesick for his own land. His wife agreed that it was time for them to leave.

They set forth on the trail and walked for many days towards the west.

"We are not far from your land," the wife said, "but we must be careful. The great shark lives near here."

Even as she spoke, the great shark swam out from behind the rocks and began to chase them. They ran as quickly as they could, but the woman began to tire. She handed their son to her husband.

"Go as quickly as you can," she said. "Keep going to the west. You will come to the beach where we first met. Do not look back. I will lead the great shark away. Wait for me and I will try to come to you."

The husband did as his wife said. He kept running towards the sun, carrying their child. The trail began to climb up a hill and he found himself on the beach in the cove where the rocks glittered brightly. He and his son waited a long time, but the wife did not return to them. Some say they are waiting there still.

Su su su su, the canoe went through the waves. Strangest of all, it was being propelled by geese attached to the sides.

Sagowenota and the Nephew of Okteondon (Seneca)

In the times long ago, an uncle and his nephew lived together in a lodge in the woods. The uncle was a very old man. He had lain so long in one spot in their lodge that the roots of an oak tree had grown over his body. He could no longer stand up, but the nephew cared for him and brought him whatever he needed.

One morning the old man called his nephew to him.

"Bring me the pouch in the corner," said the uncle. When it was brought to him, he drew forth from it packets of seeds. These he placed in small bark containers which he tied around his nephew's waist. "Now go to the field by the stream bank and sow these seeds as I tell you."

Doing as the old man said, the boy went to the field and began to plant. As he did so he thought he began to hear a song in the distance.

> I am rising
> I am rising

So the song went. But whenever he stopped planting to listen, it seemed as if the song stopped. He had almost finished the last of the seeds when he heard a great crash. It was the sound of a mighty tree falling. He ran back to the lodge and the woods and found the great tree uprooted and his uncle gone. The only traces he could find were footprints leading to the west.

Taking his bow and arrows, the nephew began to follow the trail. Three days and three nights passed as he travelled and he found himself at the edge of a huge lake. There the uncle's trail ended. Unsure of what to do, the nephew stood there looking out at the water which was calm as a ray of moonlight. Then he saw a strange sight.

Coming towards him from a great distance away across the lake was something which looked at first to be a wave. As it drew closer, though, he saw it was a canoe with a man in it. It was coming very fast. Su su su su, it went through the waves which had now formed.

Strangest of all, it was being propelled by geese attached to the sides. Now the canoe reached the shore in front of him and the young man in the canoe jumped out. He was dressed exactly like the nephew and carried a bow and arrows.

"Hongak!" shouted the young man, "go now and seek food for yourselves but return when I call." With those words, STUM! up into the sky flew the geese, leaving the canoe behind.

The young man came over to the nephew and embraced him. "Brother," he said to the nephew, "I must call you that, for you and I are the same. Look, even our bows and arrows are the same length and made of the same wood."

The nephew looked and saw it was so.

"Look also," the other one continued, "Our clothing is the same and we are of the same height."

Again the nephew looked and saw it was so. In every way the young man in the canoe looked like him.

"Tell me," said the young man. "Are you not the nephew of Okteondon?"

"Nyoh," said the nephew, "That is true."

"Ee-yah," said the other, smiling broadly, "He is my uncle also! We *are* brothers. But let's have one more test. Bend your bow as I do and shoot an arrow. Then we will run and see if we can outdistance our arrows."

Bending his bow as the other one did, the nephew shot and the other one did the same. Then both of them ran. They ran so fast that all that could be heard was the wind whipping against their sleeves, whup whup whup whup, and the clicking of the small stones of the beach thrown up by their feet, shuka shuka shuka shuka. Right past their arrows did they both run and then, reaching up at the same time as if they were images reflecting each other in the water, each of them caught the arrow they had shot.

Now the young man from the canoe seemed very happy. He led Okteondon's nephew back to his boat. "Hau," he said, "you must come with me now to a place where I play a game." He cupped his hands to his mouth and called in a loud voice, "Hongak, you who are my slaves, come back!"

Immediately, down from the sky flew the geese and attached themselves to the sides of the canoe. Climbing in, the young man motioned for Okteondon's nephew to join him and he did.

Then the young man in the canoe sang this song:

    Onen, onen, onen

    gi ne ogadendi

which means, "Now, now, now, I have started." And as he sang the geese paddled their feet and the canoe went quickly through the waves, su su su su. Before long, the nephew of Okteondon saw an island in the middle of the lake.

"There," said the other, "is the place where I play my game."

Straight to the island went the canoe until it had landed at a place on the beach where the sand showed the marks of a canoe. The young man leaped out and began to walk down the beach. "Come with me," he said to Okteondon's nephew. "Do as I do."

Along the beach they walked until they came to a large white rock which the young man from the canoe picked up and threw into the lake where the water was very deep. Down it sank, bub bub bub bub. Stripping off all his clothing, he dove in while

Okteondon's nephew watched.

After a time he came again to the surface and walked out, carrying the large white rock in his arms. "Now it is your turn to play," he said.

Wanting to please his new brother, the nephew picked up the large white stone and threw it into the water. Down it sank, bubbubbub bub. He took off all his clothing and dove in. As soon as Okteondon's nephew had disappeared below the surface, though, the other grabbed all of his clothing, ran back to the canoe and climbed in.

>Onen, onen, onen
>gi ne ogadendi

sang the other. The geese paddled with their feet and, su su su su the canoe went quickly through the waves.

When Okteondon's nephew came out of the water with the large white rock in his arms, he saw that his clothing was gone.

"Brother," he called, "where are you?" There was no answer. Casting his eyes about, he saw the canoe far out in the lake with the other in it.

"Come back for me," called Okteondon's nephew, but the other did not look at him.

Instead, the other cupped his hands and called out: "Hear me, all you who live in the water and like to eat flesh. I give you this one I have left on the island. If he comes into the water, his meat is yours."

Then, from deep in the water, Okteondon's nephew heard the sounds of the water monsters rejoicing:

> Hist hist hist hist
> hai hai hai
> Hist hist hist hist
> hai hai hai

And the canoe with the other in it went on across the water until it was out of sight.

The nephew was very miserable. "I shall die here," he said. Then he heard a very faint voice.

"Nephew," said the voice, "come over here."

Following the sound, the nephew looked over a little sandy hill. There, at its base, was the body of a man all rotted away. Little was left but bones.

"Nephew," said the rotted man, "you have been caught by the Old One, Sagowenota, the eater of human beings. This night he will come back to hunt you with his dogs. 'Twua, twua, twua,' he will call to them and they will seek you out."

"Wah-ah," said the nephew, "then it is as I thought. I will die here."

"Hau djagon," said the rotted man, "come, be brave. First give me some tobacco to smoke. My pouch is over there by that log."

Going over to the log, Okteondon's nephew found a skin pouch. Inside it was tobacco, a pipe, and a drill for making fire. Filling the pipe with tobacco, the young man made a fire, using the drill and punk from the log. Then he lit the pipe and placed it between the teeth of the rotted man.

"Ee-yah," the rotted man said, "that tobacco tastes good. Now listen to me and maybe I can help

181

you. Inside my fisher skin pouch there's a knife. Take it and carve three figures in the shape of men out of wood. Make three bows and three arrows and place them in the hands of the carved figures. Put the figures up in the three tallest trees just where they make a fork in their branches. After doing that, you must go and bury yourself in the sand where Sagowenota always beaches his canoe. Then you may be able to fool that ancient one. But before you do that, run all over the island from one place to another many times. Leave your tracks everywhere so the dogs will follow them and become confused."

"Uncle," said the nephew, "nyah-weh. I thank you for my life."

Working quickly, for the night was already coming, the young man did as he had been instructed. He made the wooden figures, placed bows and arrows in their hands, and put them high in the three trees. He laid his tracks all over the island in every direction. Then he buried himself in the sand where the Sagowenota always beached his canoe, leaving only his nose uncovered so he could breathe.

Now it was the middle of the night and the Sagowenota returned. With him in the canoe were his two fierce dogs. They were tall as a man at the shoulder and their eyes burned in the darkness like coals in a fire. All of their lives they had eaten human flesh.

As soon as the canoe pulled in, the Sagowenota leaped out and the two dogs followed.

Snidjagon, snidjagon

      hestua, hestua, hestua

he sang, which means, "You two be brave, you two be brave, there you go, there you go, there you go."

Into the darkness ran the two fierce dogs, following the tracks Okteondon's nephew had left.

All around the island they ran until the first dog came to one of the carved figures in a tree. "Wau, wau, wau," it yelped, then howled once and was silent.

"What was that?" said the Sagowenota. He ran to the place where the dog had howled. There lay his fierce dog, dead with an arrow through its chest and a carved wooden figure lying near it.

From the other side of the island the second dog yelped. "Kwen, kwen, kwen," it barked. Then it, too, howled once and was silent.

"Hunh-uh?" said the Sagowenota. He ran to the place where the second dog had howled. There it lay with an arrow through its heart and a carved wooden figure next to it on the sand. Now the Sagowenota became afraid. He turned and ran back towards the place where he had beached his canoe.

In the meantime, hearing the howls of the dogs, Okteondon's nephew had dug out from the sand and climbed into the old one's canoe.

"Onen, onen, onen," he sang to the geese, "Gi ne ogadendi," and they paddled the canoe swiftly out into the lake, su su su su through the waves.

When the Sagowenota reached the shore, he saw his canoe far out in the water.

"My brother," he called, "now our game is over.

Come back and do not leave me here."

But Okteondon's nephew did not listen. Instead he called out over the lake, "All you monsters in the water who like to eat flesh. Hear me. The one who is on the island now belongs to you."

When they heard that, the water monsters were very pleased and their song came up out of the lake.

>Hist hist hist hist
>hai hai hai
>Hist hist hist hist
>hai hai hai

On through the waves went the canoe. Now Okteondon's nephew saw another island before him. On it was a small lodge made of white birch bark.

"Hongak," he said, "stop here for a time and wait for me." Climbing out of the canoe he started for the lodge. Out of it came running a young woman.

"Brother," she said, embracing Okteondon's nephew, "You have escaped the ancient one. I am your sister whom our Uncle sought before he was killed by the Sagowenota. Here are your bow and arrows and the clothing which the old one took from you. Now we must hurry before he tries to catch us."

With a hatchet made of flint in her hand, the nephew's sister climbed with him back into the canoe. Once more he gave the geese the command to go and as they paddled through the waves he sang this song:

>Onen onen onen
>gi ne sagadendi

which means, "Now, now now, I again start homeward."

At first their canoe went swiftly, su su su su, but then it began to slow down until it stood still in the water, no matter how hard the geese paddled. The nephew urged them on, but the canoe stood as if frozen in ice.

"The Sagowenota is trying to pull us back," said the sister. She leaned over to look beneath the canoe. There, sure enough, was a hook with a line fastened to it stuck in the bottom of the canoe. Taking the flint hatchet she struck the hook and dislodged it. Once again they went quickly through the water, su su su su.

They had almost reached the shore when the boat again stood still in the water. The sister looked back.

"Look," she cried, "The Sagowenota is drinking all of the water in the lake to draw us back to him!"

Okteondon's nephew looked back. Now they were moving backwards towards the island. He could see the Sagowenota down on his knees with his mouth in the water, drawing all of the lake into his belly. Larger and larger the Sagowenota's belly grew until it looked as large as the island itself. Drawing his bow, Okteondon's nephew took aim and let his arrow fly, straight into the Sagowenota's paunch it flew, piercing it and letting all of the water free in a great wave which lifted the canoe, the geese and the two passengers, carrying them to the other shore.

Stepping out of the canoe, the young man turned to the geese. "Hongak," he said, "our Creator did not intend you to be the slaves of another. I set you free." Then STUM! all of the geese flew up into the sky, never again to be servants, as Okteondon's nephew and the sister went happily along their way. Ever since then, though, because the geese remember how it was when they pulled the canoe of Sagowenota, they still fly together in formation through the skies.

Da neho nigagais. That is how long this story is.

From that day on, the longhouse of Jigonsahseh would be known as the Peace House. All would now call her the Yegowaneh, "The Mother of Nations."

The Mother of Nations
(Neutral)

Long ago there was a woman whose longhouse stood to the west at Oniagara. Her people, whom she led, were those known as the Cultivators, the Hadiyent-togeo-no and they were cousins to the Ongwe-oweh.

It was said that this woman was the direct descendent of the first woman born on the Earth. Her name was Jigonsahseh, the Lynx. Her longhouse stood by the warriors' path which ran from east to west. Though she was unable to stop the continual war which tore apart the nations in those days, still her words were respected. She always fed those who passed her door and she was called by many "The Great Mother."

When The Peacemaker, who brought the great message from the Master of Life, set out into the world he went first to the land of the Cultivators. He crossed Sganya-dai-yo, the Great Beautiful Lake, in his canoe made of white stone. He saw that there

188

were no cornfields planted because of the continual warfare. The towns were stockaded and filled with people who were hungry and quarrelling.

The Peacemaker went to the house of Jigonsahseh. She welcomed him and placed food before him. When he had finished eating she spoke. "You have come to bring a message," she said. "My mind is open to it. I wish to hear."

Then The Peacemaker spoke. He told her he was acting as the messenger of the Maker of Life. He said that his message was to bring justice, peace, and good laws for the people. The wars between the Ongwe-oweh, the True Human Beings, would cease.

"This message is good," said Jigonsahseh. "What form shall it take among the People?"

Then The Peacemaker explained. "It will take the form of the Longhouse. There will be many fires within the Longhouse, many families. But all will live together under the guidance of a wise Clan Mother. The five nations of the Ongwe-oweh will become of one mind and be known as the People of the Longhouse. Together they will seek the way of Peace which would be open to all the nations."

"My hands are open to this message. I reach out and grasp it," said Jigonsahseh.

Then it was decided that, since a woman was the first to accept this new way, from that day on the women would possess the titles and give them to the men who would speak for their nations in the Longhouse. These women would name from their clans the men who would serve the people. The

Clan Mothers would give them the horns of office and if they did not do their jobs well the women could take back their titles.

From that day on, the longhouse of Jigonsahseh would be known as the Peace House. All would now call her the Yegowaneh, "The Mother of Nations." In the land of her people there would be no war. The Cultivators would now be known as the Attiwendaronk, "The Neutral Nation."

So it came to be that in the land of the Yegowaneh, the Mother of Nations, there was no war. Her name was passed down from mother to eldest daughter. When it was necessary for the People of the Longhouse to deal with other nations who had not joined the League of Peace or when there were disputes between nations, the War Captains would always pass first through her land and deliver Peace Belts to the Yegowaneh.

She would give them food, as had been the custom of all those who carried the name of Jigonsahseh and were descended from the first woman born on Earth. Then the Mother of Nations would exhort them to seek peace and accept war only as a last resort. So it is said among the People of the Longhouse that the path of war runs through the House of Peace.

The longer the young man looked at the seven stones,
the more they looked like old men.

The Seven Mateínnu (Lenape)

Long ago, there were seven *mateinnu*. These men had grown very wise after years of fasting and dreaming. They had been blessed with power from The Great *Manito*, The Creator. They knew the herbs for curing and were able to do many things to help the people. They could often see things which were about to happen and tell people what to do to prepare. However, because the seven *mateinnu* were so wise, everyone came to them to ask for help. People began demanding so much of them that the wise men finally decided to hide themselves so that they would have some peace.

"Everyone knows what we look like," said one of the *mateinnu*. "How can we conceal ourselves?"

"Let us change ourselves into rocks of different shapes," said another of the wise men. Then, because they had such power, they did just that. They became seven large stones and the people passed by them without knowing who they really were.

So things continued for a long time. In the village, though, there was a young man with very good eyes. This young man always saw the things which others missed and he also paid close attention to his dreams and tried to lead a good life. One night a dream came to him and told him to go to the place in the forest where there were seven stones and look closely. The next morning, the young man did just that. He went to the place where the seven stones were and looked at them very closely. The longer he looked at them the more they looked like old men. Finally, the young man leaned close to one of the stones.

"Grandfather," said the young man, "are you well?"

"Yes, Grandson," answered the stone. "Thank you for asking."

Then the young man began to speak with the stone. Soon the other stones, which had been silent for a long time, joined into the conversation. They told the young man things which would be useful for his people and when he returned to the village he was able to do good deeds with his new knowledge. The next day he went again to talk with the seven *mateinnu*.

So things went for a time. Then others from the village began following the young man and saw where he went. They observed him speaking to the stones and realized the seven stones were the seven lost wise men. Now others came to the stones and tried to speak to them. The stones would speak only to that young man who had looked closely enough to see them, but they were bothered by all the visitors. Finally, when the young man came alone to see them one day, the *mateinnu* changed back into human shape.

"Grandfathers," said the young man, "I am glad to see you."

"Thank you, Grandson," said the seven *mateinnu*. "But we have taken our human shapes once more because we are going away. As it was before, the people are giving us no peace. Use the knowledge we have given you well."

Then the seven wise men went away. It is said that they went further into the forest and changed themselves into seven cedar trees. They were trees of such perfect shape and size, though, that before long people noticed them and decided they were the seven wise men. They began to come to the place where the *mateinnu* were in the shape of trees. They came in such numbers that once again the seven *mateinnu* had no peace. That was when The Great Manito took pity on the *mateinnu*. He lifted them up into the sky and changed them into the stars. To this day you can see them, the stars the Lenape call The Seven Wise Men, The Pleiades.

THE WALUM OLUM

The Walum Olum (a name which means "Red Score" in the language of the Lenape), is an epic poem recorded in pictographs. Recorded on birch bark or painted on wooden sticks, such picture writing was more common throughout Native North America than most realize. Many of the pictographs, in fact, seem to have similar meanings throughout the continent and there are distinct similarities to the complex pictographic language of the Aztecs and Maya of Mexico. One of the towns in central New York State, Painted Post, gained its name from the many wooden markers covered with Iroquois pictographs which used to stand where the town was built. As was the case with the thousands of actual books written by the Aztec and Maya, books destroyed by the Spanish as "works of the devil," much of the pictographic tradition was destroyed soon after the arrival of the Europeans. *The Walum Olum* itself only survives because of one European scholar, Constantine Samuel Rafinesque, who copied the pictographs from the original wooden records, transcribed the Delaware verses as they were spoken to him by a Lenape informant, and then did a rough translation of them. In 1836, Rafinesque published *The Walum Olum* as a part of his larger study of the American Nations.

Several studies and retranslations of *The Walum Olum* have been done over the years. The two best are Daniel Garrison Brinton's *The Lenape and their Legends* (1954), which is an excellent work of serious scholarship, including glyphs, Lenape and literal translations, and Joe Napora's *The Walum Olum* (1983), which contains only the glyphs and a lively, more poetic English translation.

In the words of Joe Napora,

An epic is the "tale of the tribe. *The Walum Olum* is such a tale. It is the only North American epic poem that we know to have existed before Columbus. It is perhaps the only pictographic epic poem. It is unique. And yet it is representative of a large body of literature that has been ignored by the purveyors of taste for what passes for culture on this continent.

The following pages comprise only the first two parts of the poem. There are 136 more glyphs, telling of the history and migrations of the Lenape and ending with the coming of the Europeans.

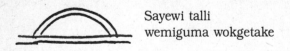 Sayewi talli
wemiguma wokgetake

At first, in that place
at all times,
above the earth.

Hackung kwelik
owanaku
wak yutali
Kitanitowit-essop

Mist extended
over the earth
and there
the great Manito was.

Sayewis hallemiwis
nolemiwi
elemamik
Kitanitowit-essop

At first, forever,
there and not there
everywhere and
nowhere
the great Manito was.

Sohawalawak kwelik
hakik
woak awasagamak

He made land here
He made sky there

Sohalawak gishuk
nipaham alankwak

He made the sun
made moon and stars

Wemi-sohalawak
yulikyuchaan

He made them all
move evenly,
moving within them

197

Wich-owagan kshakan
moshaguat
kwelik kshipehelep

A hard wind blew
and it cleared
and the water flowed
strong to the many
places.

Opeleken mani-menak
delsin-epit

Many islands grew in
groups and remained

Lappinup Kitanitowit
manito manitoak

Then Manito spoke
a manito to manitos

Owiniwak an-
gelatawiwak
chichankwak wemiwak

making many beings
speaking breath into
them

Wtenk manito jinwis
lennowak mukom

and forever he is Manito
Grandfather to us all

Milap netami gaho
owini gaho

he gives to us all
First Mother, mother of
us all

Nanesik Milap, tulpewik
milap
awesik milap, cholensak
milap

he gives fish, gives
turtles,
gives four-leggeds,
gives birds

Makimani shak so-
halawak
makowini makowak
amangamek

But an evil manito
makes Water Snake
makes Black Snake

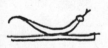

Shukand eli-kimi
mekenikink
wakon powako init'ako

But in secret, Great
Snake
came among them

Mattalogas pallalogas
maktaton
owagan payat-chik
yutali

he brought with him all
sorts of badness,
quarreling and meanness

199

Maktapan payat
wihillan payat
mboagan payat

brought bad weather
brought sickness
brought death

Won wemi wiwunch
kamik
atak kitahikan
netamaki epit

All this took place
on Old Earth
in the time beyond
the great tide-waters

Wulamo maskanako
anup
lennowak makowini
essopak

In this time of the
mighty snake
and powerful men

Maskanako shingalusit
nijini
essopak shawelendamep
eken shingalan

this mighty snake
hated them
and fought with the
people

Nishawi palliton
Nishawi machiton
Nishawi matta lun-
gundowin

both did harm to each
other
both did injury to each
other
both were not in peace

Mattapewi wiki ni-
hanlowit
mekwazoan

driven from their
homes
they fought this
dead-maker

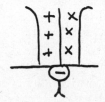

Sohalawak uchewak
sohalawak pungusak

he makes the
mosquitoes
he makes the punkies

Nitisak wemi owini
w'delisinewuap

this was a time of
friendship
and harmony between
all

Kiwis wunuad
wishimanitoak
essopak

truly, all the manitos
were kind and in
balance

Nujini netami lennowak
nigoha netami okwewi,
nanitewak

to those first men
seeking
the first women were
brought
brought to each other
the women and men

Gattamin netami mitzi
nijini nantini

and when they first
desired food
berries were brought to
them

Wemi wingi-namenep
Wemi ksin-elendamep
Wemi wullatemanuwi

All had useful
knowledge
All had leisure
All had good thinking

Maskanako gishi
penauwelendamep
lennowak owini palliton

The Great Snake
decided
to harm the people

Nakowa petonep
amangam petonep
akopehella petonep

Three persons he
brought,
whirlwind he brought,
rushing water he
brought

Pehella pehella
pohoka pohoka
eshohok eshohok
palliton palliton

water rushing, water
rushing
to the hills, to the hills
penetrating, penetrating
destroying, destroying

Tulapit menapit
Nanaboush
maskaboush
owinimokan
linowimokan

Strong one Nanabush
Grandfather of beings
Grandfather of people
was on the Turtle Island

Gishikin-pommixin
tulagishatten lohxin

There he was walking,
creating
There he made the
Turtle

Owini linowi wemoltin
Pehella gahani
pommixin
Nahiwi tatalli tulapin

Four-leggeds and two
leggeds
went forth, walked in
high water
walked in low water.
walked downstream
to the Turtle Island

Amanganek mak-
dopannek
alendyuwek met-
zipannek

Monster fishes came
ate some of them

Manito-dasin mokol-
wichemap
Palpal payat payat
wemichemap

Manito daughter came
helped with her canoe
helped as
as they came and came

Nanaboush, Nanaboush
wemimokom
Wimimokom lin-
nimokom
tulamokom

Nanabush, Nanabush
Grandfather of all
Grandfather of animal
people
Grandfather of humans
Grandfather of the Turtle

Linapi-ma tulapi-ma
tulapewi tapitawi

Lenapi people
together now on the
Turtle
Turtle-men on the
Turtle

Wishanem tulpewi
pataman tulpewi
poniton wuliton

Frightened on the
Turtle
they prayed on the
Turtle
Prayed for the cleansing
of what was spoiled

Ksipehelen penkwihelen
Kwamipokho sitwalikho
Maskan wagan palliwi
palliwi

Water ran off
Earth dried
still water and silence
Mighty snake goes away
goes away

Glossary

Abenaki: The People of the Dawn Land, literally "Dawn Land People," or Wabanakiak. Approximately thirteen different but related Native American nations in the areas now known as Vermont, New Hampshire, Maine and parts of Canada. The name may also refer to the western Abenaki people, sometimes known as "St. Francis Abenaki," because they live near the St. Francis River in Quebec.

Algonquin: Refers to both the language family which encompasses the languages of many different native nations (Anishinabe, Abenaki, Lenape, Mohegan, etc.) and to certain native peoples of Canada called "Algonquin."

Anishinabe: Native American peoples also known as Chippewa or Ojibway. Their home land is in the Great Lakes region. "Anishinabe" means "first or original people." "Ojibway" or "Chippewa" is a name which their neighbors used to refer to them: "o-jib-weg," or "those who make pictographs."

Dah-joh: Welcome or Come in. (Iroquois)

Dah-neh hoh: Story ending meaning "that is all." (Iroquois)

Gah-ka: Crow. (Iroquois)

Gitchee Manitou: "Great Spirit," or "Great Mystery," the creator. (Anishinabe)

Glooskap: The transformer and trickster hero of the Wabanaki, also called "Koluscap" or "Gluskabe" or "Klooskap." His name means "Storyteller" or "Talker."

Iroquois: The Five Nations and, after 1722, Six Nations of people who formed a Great League of Peace which encompassed an area larger than the Roman Empire. They called themselves the Hau-de-no-sau-nee, or Hotinnonsionni, the "People of the Extended House." The name "Iroquois" apparently came from an Algonquin language and may have meant "enemies." The Six Nations of the Iroquois were:

Nundawaono: People of the Great Hill (Seneca)
Gueugwehonono: The Mucky Land People (Cayuga)
Onundagaono: The People on the Hills (Onondaga)
Onayotakaono: The Standing Stone People (Oneida)
Ganeagaono: The Flint Place People (Mohawk)
Dusgaoweh: The Shirt-Wearing People (Tuscarora)

Iroquoian: The family of languages which includes those languages spoken by the Six Nations, the Cherokees, the Hurons, Neutrals and many others.

Kiwakweskwa: a female cannibal giant. (Abenaki)

Ktaadan: Khta'-adena', which means "Great Mountain." (Abenaki)

Ktchiawassak: "Giant animals." (Abenaki)

Kweh: Hello. (Abenaki)

Kwe-yoh: An expression of excitement or displeasure. (Abenaki)

Lenape: An Algonquin-speaking people also known as the Delawares. Found in the area now known as Pennsylvania, New Jersey and Southern New York (including the area of New York City), they called themselves Lenape, "ordinary people" or "real people." The name "Delaware" was given them by the whites and comes from the Delaware River, named after Lord De la Warr, the first Governor of Virginia. Many were forced to relocate many times in the 1700s and 1800s, with the results that settlements of Lenape People today are found in New Jersey, in Oklahoma and in Canada.

Mahican: People found in area south from Lake Champlain along the Hudson River. Forced to move many times, their descendents are found among the Stockbridge-Munsee Indians of Wisconsin. Their name derived from "Muhheakunnuck," referring to the ebb and flow of the Hudson River tidal waters.

Manansis: "Island which is small." (Abenaki)

Mateguas: Rabbit. (Abenaki)

Mesatawe: "Morning Star." (Abenaki)

Micmac: The Northeasternmost of the Wabanaki peoples. Their lands are what are now known as the Maritime Provinces and Gaspe penisula of Canada. Their name is usually interpreted to mean "allies." Their outlook on life (and that of many of the other Native people of the Northeastern Woodlands) was summarized by Philip Bock as based on the following five ideas: 1) Life is everywhere, visible and invisible and various forms of life may change into one another. 2) The ancestors were great hunters, strong, dignified, healthy, generous, just, and brave. 3) Indians have powers different from other people, such things as spirit helpers and "Indian luck." 4) People are equal, or should be. No one should put himself above others. 5) Moderation is better than excess.

Mohegan: An Algonquin people living along the coast of what is now western Connecticut. Their name means "Wolf People."

Mondawmin: Anishinabe spirit of the corn.

Nanabush: The trickster hero of many Anishinabe stories.

Nda: No. (Abenaki)

Neh: No. (Iroquois)

Neutral: A group of allied Iroquoian nations located between the Hurons and the Five Nations Iroquois who remained Neutral in the wars between the Hurons and Iroquois. One of the nations closest to the Senecas, which was later absorbed by the Seneca, was the Wenro, which means "People of the place of floating moss."

Niaweh: Thank you. (Seneca)

Nyoh: Yes. (Iroquois)

Onondaga: One of the Six Nations of the Iroquois. Their home lands are in what is now central New York, near Syracuse. They were the fire-keepers of the Iroquois league and also the custodian of the record-keeping wampum belts for the League. Their name means "People on the Hill," an apt description of the hilly valley where the Onondaga Reservation still exists.

Passamaquoddy: One of the Wabanaki nations located in what is now eastern Maine. Their name means "Those of the place where pollock fish are plentiful," and it reflects their reliance upon the sea for their livelihood.

Penobscot: One of the Wabanaki nations located in the area now known as central Maine. Their name means "where the rocks widen."

Podawawogan: "Whale which is blowing." (Abenaki)

Sagowenota: A monster associated with the tides. (Iroquois)

Seneca: The westernmost of the Six Iroquois nations, they called themselves Nunda-wa-ono, "the people of the Great Hill," a name reflecting their belief that they originated from the top of a large hill. The name "Seneca" is apparently a corruption of an Algonquin word "Osin-in-ka" meaning "People of the stone."

Skanoh: Peace. (Niaweh skanoh: "I greet you in peace.") Iroquois

Skunny-Wundy: "Cross the creek." (Iroquois)

Sokoki: One of the westernmost Abenaki nations. Means "Those who broke away."

Tuscarora: The last of the Six Nations of the Iroquois to join the league. Originally located in the area now known as North Carolina, they were forced by warfare and betrayal by the whites, to migrate north where they were given refuge by the Iroquois League in 1713 and were formally adopted into the League around 1722.

Unh-hunh: Yes. (Abenaki)

Walum Olum: "Red Score," the record of the tale of the Creation and the history of the Lenape people recorded on pieces of wood in pictographs.

Wampum: the purple and white shells of the quahog clam which were shaped into beads and strung together to make record belts which carried messages and served as records of treaties and other agreements between the Native American peoples and between them and the whites. Wampum was later used by Europeans for a time as a form of currency, due to its great value among Indian people.

About the Author

A poet and teacher, Joe Bruchac has been writer-in-residence at Hamilton College, Columbia University, and numerous local libraries and Indian reservation schools, as well as teaching Native American literature at the State University of New York at Albany. Featured as a storyteller at festivals in New York, Vermont, Illinois, Missouri, Massachusetts, Nevada, and England, he was brought to Alaska in May 1987 by the Institute of Alaska Native Arts to work with native storytellers from Juneau to Barrow. A Black Belt in the martial arts, he has worked for a number of years as an instructor of Pentjak Silat.

Paul J. Horton

About the Illustrator

"It was a pleasure to bring to life talking rocks, giants, and adventures with our animal friends. It was a privilege to share with Native Americans their sensitivity and respect for nature."

Gary Carpenter is an illustrator-graphic designer as well as a professional musician. He lives with his wife Karen and two cats in Santa Cruz, CA.